The World Around Us

by Barbara Vogel

Those Around Us

by

Barbara Vogel

Cover Design by Eric Murillo
Interior Design by Eric Murillo
Illustration by Stephanie Welsh

Published by Barbara Vogel
Paperback ISBN: 978-1-952421-19-8

First Edition
Printed in the United States.

Acknowledgements

I want to give my deepest thanks to Andrea Petry for her helpfulness in bringing this book to publication. She went above and beyond what any friend would do. She kept me grounded and always steered me in the right direction. You were so patient and deserve sainthood due to all my questions. You are a good friend indeed.

Thank you, Heather Josi, for your wonderful editing ability.

Many thanks to Cecilia Ramos for your insight, discernment and great advice.

I also want to thank my daughter, Selene Nesland, for your help and encouragement.

Thank you Regi Da Silva for your invaluable feedback.

If you are searching for the supernatural, you will find it. Be assured, that the amazing Force that created you always sees you, and you are loved.

Chapter One

LET ME INTRODUCE MYSELF. MY NAME IS SUSAN QUADE. And yes I have been called Susie Q. many times. Everyone thinks they are the originator of this hilarious joke; except I am not laughing. But whatever floats your boat. There are many other names that people could call me that I would object to, even more vehemently.

And there are many names that I would call myself. Clumsy and ungraceful, are among the many names. Not that I am putting a word curse upon myself, but I am just telling the truth. And I do not consider myself very pretty, but I'm not ugly. In fact, I don't know many women that consider themselves beautiful. Why is that? Do we compare ourselves to the Vogue models? Does society put that expectation or desire on us? Whether it does or not, I do desire to be beautiful. And since I am making a wish list, I would like to be wanted, desired, and loved. And I also want to put on the list, graceful, wealthy, and skinny (with the ability to eat anything I want without gaining a pound). And how about ripped!

11

A woman-like six pack would work in the fabulous category, without any exercise.

This is my life of daydreaming. Instead, I go to work every day on the bus to a downtown office building in the large West Coast city of Portland, Oregon. Portland is a beautiful city with a diverse population. This city has many bridges crossing over two different rivers that meander through the area. At night, the bridges light up with different colors and you can just imagine yourself walking over the bridge with your beloved, arm in arm. But instead, I look through my office window and only daydream. I dream of a safe community where you can walk arm in arm with anyone and not be hassled, pan handled, or intimidated.

This day starts like any other rainy Monday. It is always raining in Portland and this is the autumn season where the rain starts and does not end until July. Seriously! We have just gotten over the 'Indian summer' which ends in October and we are getting in the mode of "this is our life now." We wear raincoats with hoods or carry an umbrella. To tell you the truth, the long-time residents of Portland rarely put up an umbrella unless they are wearing a business suit. We either make a run for it or put up our hoods and mildly take a stroll through the water slogged streets. You can always spot the foreigner, they have an umbrella up. They have obviously not grown up in this demographic area of wetness.

I work for a prestigious attorney firm and my boss is the lead attorney for the organization. I had just finished a long Monday workday of catching up from the past week and I was preparing for the upcoming week's heavy workload. I was exhausted from all the mental gymnastics of trying to second-guess what my boss needed. His verbal skills are minimal, unless he is in a court room. Usually in the office, he has a style of nonverbal communication that is directed to anyone beneath his stature when he communicates, but not in a mean way. He would say, "I thought I told you this?" "No, you did not." And he does not believe you. His mind is racing so fast that he does not realize that he did not speak it out. I am getting pretty good at noticing his cues, anticipating his next move and trying to stay one step ahead of what he needs next. It reminds me of the old television show, M*A*S*H. Radar O'Reilly always anticipated the camp commander's needs, to the point of finishing his sentences. Radar is my hero. I know my boss does appreciate these skills that I have, even if he does not compliment me.

At the beginning of the week, I am trying to stay one step of my boss and plan the rest of the week so that I can begin to jump through the hoops of mind reading of my boss. It can be exhausting but it is a job that I like because of the challenges. As I exit my building, after finishing my workday, I look up into the dark rainclouds. It has been sprinkling all day with the occasional downpours and it looks like it will rain buckets in just a second. I take the bus to work which means that I will be standing in the rain waiting for my bus to arrive. We have shelters to stand under but at this time of day, with everyone getting off work, they will be filled. And as I look down the street at my bus stop, my prediction is correct.

I slosh through the puddle and feel the wetness seep into my sock. Dang, I forgot this boot was coming apart from the sole. At least it is happening at the end of my day instead of the morning. I need to keep my thoughts optimistic. As I wait for my bus to come thundering down the street, I try to turn my thoughts off from the workday and turn my thoughts towards the evening. It is a mental exercise that I try to do so that I do not take home what the mental and emotion climate of the downtown encompasses. This "climate" includes my work, my lunchtime interaction with friends in the office, any of the homeless that I see on the streets, and any clients that I have interacted with. I try to start this exercise at the bus stop and continue until I reach my neighborhood. It is a training of acknowledgement and putting it aside, and file it away in a file cabinet in my mind. It can be accessible for later. I just go to the file cabinet in my mind and pull out the thought pattern. It is like a photographic memory, which I do not have, but my filing system never goes away. I remember everything that is important and that is why my boss loves me so much. I can access these brain files at any time. Actually, I guess I don't remember everything... I forgot about my boot leaking. But that was from last year when it rained in the spring. Boots are not worth remembering.

I see my number 43 bus coming from a couple of blocks down. It is behind a line of cars that are weaving in and out of traffic. I anticipate the shift that will happen underneath the shelter as people move out and others push in towards the dry area. I prepare to take out my bus pass, shifting my purse and lunch bag, and get ready to move forward. The bus begins to pull over with a huge splash of water onto the sidewalk. Everyone groans as the wave hits them. People begin to politely shove forward and as I approach the bus, I feel a push from behind and I go tumbling forward. My feet are unable to keep up with the forward motion of what my body was making. I'm falling quickly without a steady empty hand to catch me. In slow motion, I think "this is gonna hurt."

Just then, a hand shoots out and catches my coat and pulls me upright and steadies me. I was shocked at the abruptness of it. I look around in disbelief and there is a young woman standing there smiling. She had blond shoulder length hair, and a round beautiful face with these gorgeous eyes that you could just melt into. Her skin was translucent, in a good way, and her complexion was flawless. I stood there with my mouth hanging open. I stammered a thank you.

"Are you a weightlifter? I was falling and you just yanked me back onto my feet," I inquired.

She giggled. Who giggles now-a-days?

"I know that I can be a bit clumsy, but I felt that I was shoved from behind. I am certainly glad you were there to catch me. I really appreciate your quick action." I was trying to straighten my jacket that was askew and then I began to pick up my things that had fallen onto the sidewalk. And she just stood there smiling.

After I pulled myself together, I realized that we were standing on the sidewalk alone and the bus had loaded up the passengers and had gone on its way. Oh crap, I will need to wait another twenty minutes for the next bus to come. My face must have registered the frustration because she had knotted up her eyebrows in a curious manner. I explained that I would have to wait for the next bus. I asked her if she was waiting for the same bus as I? She shook her head no. I thought to ask her why she was there, when she abruptly smiled and walked away.

Barbara Vogel

I watched her as she strolled away, down the sidewalk. There was a honk from the street and a screech of tires. I took my eyes off her for just a second to see where the screech came from and when I returned my gaze, she was already gone. Gosh, I forgot to get her name. Boy, I was really thankful that she was there to catch me. It could have been disastrous. I could imagine a hurt shoulder, or scraped face, or a bump on the head. I noticed that it had stopped raining. Thank goodness for that.

My bus came and I thoughtfully chewed on the events that had just happened. She was a pleasant looking young woman and I could imagine her with tons of boyfriends. And she seemed nice. I bet she does not go home to an empty house. Empty. No pets and no roommates. I like the calmness of my house. I am with people all day long and I like the quietness that my home entails. I have my friends over whenever I want, or I go out. But I am an introvert and I like my alone time. I spend my time reading or watching a little bit of television. I like detective shows or books where I can figure out the 'who done it' before the disclosure at the end. I also love travel shows and to see interesting places. I have plenty of friends that keep me busy on the weekends or I will take a road trip in my car. I love to travel, and it doesn't matter on what mode of transportation. I have no fear about traveling by myself, even if it is international destinations.

When I got home, I fixed myself something to eat and turned on the TV so that I could turn off my mind from the events of the day. I turned on the travel channel that was featuring a segment on Italy. I had been there a couple of years ago and I have always desired to go back. I had just graduated college and I had treated myself to the trip. As I watched the show, I drifted off to sleep. I awoke at two o'clock in the morning with a stiff neck. I don't know what awoke me, but I remember feeling unsettled. I got ready for bed, even though I would be getting up soon. I took two Ibuprofen for my stiff neck and quickly fell into a deep sleep.

The rest of my week was mundane. Nothing new but I was anticipating the weekend. I was taking off with a friend and traveling up to Seattle's Pike Place Market. It was going to be just a day trip since Seattle is only 3 hours away. I love Seattle with its bay views and watching the ferry boats go in and out of the docks. The smell of the sea and the stink of the fish are exhilarating. I know it sounds crazy. I love to go to the fish vendor inside the Market and watch the fish throwers. These guys will throw whole salmon over the heads of the onlookers and across the marketplace. It is great to experience it and I never have seen them drop a fish yet. The marketplace has all kinds of shops and knick-knacks. There is a fabulous crepe place in the market that is to die for. My mouth begins to water just anticipating the delicate French pancake that will hit my taste buds. Yum.

The end of the week rolls around and I give Dawn, my friend, a call and ask what time she wanted to leave in the morning. She groans at the fact that she has double booked herself. Her cousin has shown up the day before, unannounced. Her cousin was having marriage problems and our trip plan just fell out of her mind. Dawn apologizes profusely and we say that we will reschedule another time. I feel my shoulders slump. I was really looking forward to our trip to Seattle. Well, why can't I just go anyway? Yeah why not! I am my best company anyway, with a snort of laughter.

Barbara Vogel

I get up early and check the weather for the Seattle area. It is going to be just cloudy with no anticipation of rain. This day gets better and better. I fill up my gas tank and I roll out onto Interstate 5 north. When I found out that Dawn couldn't go, I decided to download a book to listen to while I drove. It was a fiction book about Israel. I love World War II period novels, and this seemed like it could be interesting. There are times that I go to the library and just grab anything off the shelf. Some days I have hit the jackpot with an interesting book and then there are days that I hit a dud. Well, let's see what I got.

As I drive up the freeway, my mind began to be absorbed in this beautiful tale of survival that the Jews face in this new homeland of Israel, that is not exactly theirs yet. They are still under the British Mandate which was about to expire. With the British leaving the area, it created a black hole of who was going to occupy the land. The Jews say that it is theirs from their ancient history, going all the way back to King David, and also the promise that Britain gave them in 1917 to establish a national home for the Jewish people in Palestine. But there were many forces that did not want this to happen, which included some of the British people and the surrounding Arab and Palestinian inhabitants. The book throws in a romance just to keep it interesting. The Jewish refugees that have survived the war wanted to go into this new homeland but are prevented from coming into the land. The League of Nations restricted the Jewish immigration due largely to the objections of the Arabs. The exodus of refugees from Europe to be smuggled into Palestine became very dangerous. The British would intercept most ships of the Holocaust survivors and would send them back to Europe for further persecution or to be interned into detention camps. To be returned to Poland where

18

there were ongoing pogroms of violence happening was obviously not a good thing.

So this edge of the seat thriller that was unfolding in my car, kept my attention riveted, and the miles flew by on the interstate. Before I knew it, I was driving into downtown Seattle and heading toward the market and what they lovingly call "the Sound." It actually is called the Puget Sound in the Pacific Northwest. It is truly a lovely site of scenic coast-lines and so much green as you look out over the bay. With all of our rain, how could it not be green? The sun was just peeking out from the clouds and the air was crisp but not cold. I had on tennis shoes and jeans and had opted out of boots, because of the "no rain" prediction. I layered myself with a t-shirt, with a sweater over the top, and a jacket to carry for the evening. I could feel the excitement in my cells of my body. I could feel myself smiling and I noticed people were returning my smile. There was a crowd of shoppers already at the market. When the sun comes out, everyone else comes out too. The sun can just woo you out of any household.

My first stop is the coffee shop, Seattle's Best Coffee. I love this brand and anticipate the aroma of a stiff black cup. I bought a slice of banana bread to go along with the coffee. That should ease the hunger pains, until the crepe place opened for the lunch hour. I sat on an outside bench, just outside the market, enjoying the sea air and sipped coffee. I took a deep breath and felt a cleansing in my inner soul. This felt really nice. I sipped and people-watched. This is my very favorite thing to do, to observe human behavior and their little idiosyncrasies. It can be quite entertaining.

My banana bread was now in my tummy and I was almost done with my coffee. I was trying to decide which floor I was going to conquer at the market. Suddenly, from across the street, I was mentally pulled in that direction. I swiveled my head quickly and I saw a familiar face. It's that girl from the bus stop! She was standing there just looking at me. She smiled and turned to walk away. Wait! I literally dropped my coffee cup and started running across the street. I had to stop for a car that nearly sideswiped me and when I looked again, she was gone. No!!! I cannot believe my eyes. I started looking all over the street, down between the vegetable booths and down an alley. I couldn't see her anywhere. Where the heck could she have disappeared to? I felt this sadness envelope around me and felt like a failure. Why couldn't I have been a little faster?

For the rest of the day, I looked around constantly as I shopped. I was hoping I could see her again. I don't know why I felt this urgency to connect with her, but I did. Of all things! To see her in Seattle! I wondered if she was a Seattle native or a Portland resident? Another missed opportunity. Drat!

It was a wonderful day, despite this disappointment. I do talk to God occasionally and I felt that I needed to say something now. "Lord, I wish I was able to talk to that girl."

Chapter Two

MY WEEKS DRONED ON INTO A RITUALISTIC ROUTINE.
Nothing new happened throughout the month of November, except for
Thanksgiving, one of my favorite holidays. I usually go to my parent's
house with my sister and brother attending. All of the siblings are un-
married, much to my parents' chagrin. I believe they wished their kids
would get settled and be checked off their worry list. My mother is a
worrier, and my father would rather bury his head behind the newspaper
or computer. Dad would pop his head up if there was something important to interject but that was not very often.

My older brother, Jeffrey, is a pastor in a conservative non-denominational church in town. I don't attend his church, not because he is my
brother, but because it is clear across town. But for the few times that
I have attended, it was hilarious to watch the young ladies strive for his
attention. The handsome pastor had his following, like a Pied Piper, in a
good way. It reminded me of the American Kennel Club pet parade. The

dogs were primped and polished, fluffed and manicured for the showing, and ready to be paraded around. The first time I went to visit his congregation, after he was installed as their pastor, I was amazed at the looks I received from the ladies that considered me as competition. Especially since I purposely went up and gave him a hug. I know that it was ornery of me to do that, but I did get a kick out of it. I guess it's the rebel in me.

My younger sister, Mary, is a whole different ball of wax. She is all about personal freedom and doing what she wants. She is "one with the universe." A basic tree-hugger and save-the-whales kinda gal. Of course there is nothing wrong with either of those things, but her contributions to society are tethered to organizations that are radicalized. She would label herself as a "free-thinker" even though she follows other people's mandates. She would classify herself as a holistic, universalist, spiritualist but I just put her into a category of New Age to make it easier on my own mind. I usually stay out of her discussions with my brother since they can become heated at times. I consider myself neutral when it comes to their disputes. They ask my opinion and I just say, "Switzerland."

It's not that I do not have an opinion when it comes to their religious discussions, but it's more that I feel that I am inadequate to form an opinion or put my finger on my own belief systems. My parents were not really church goers, except during special occasions. I liked church when I was young child and I especially liked the youth group meetings (there were some hot guys that went to that church). But I wouldn't say I had a staunch belief system. I believe in God that lives in heaven and I also know there is evil in the world. I only needed to go to work for that to be a reality. Seriously, I have not experienced pure evil but I know that it exists. You only need to read about Hitler, Heinrich Himmler, Joseph Stalin, Idi Amin, or the Ayatollah Khomeini of Iran to name only a few. I would classify them as evil men. But I still wrestled with the thought of how God could let evil reign on the earth. He is an all-powerful being and I wondered why He could not just snap His fingers and say, "No more."

Our Thanksgiving would begin with well-meaning intentions of thankfulness. Mom would make a huge turkey dinner with all the trimmings, a variety of potatoes, sweet and mashed, gravy from the drippings, salads, and rolls with real butter. I was usually asked to bring a vegetable dish which was alternated between green bean casserole or cheesy corn casserole. My brother was the designated drinks person (I think mom felt sorry for him that he didn't have a wife to cook for him) and my sis was the dessert person, which one year she brought yogurt. She received such grief over that one that she shaped up after that and brought real desserts. Dinner was laid out onto the extended table, and as we were dishing up, we were discussing our previous few weeks. My grandmother would pipe up with her rare opinions.

Grandmom, what a wonder she is. She was my father's mother and was quiet a force to be reckoned with. She was stoic, logical, and a powerful church going prayer warrior. She was proud that her grandson was a pastor and was also a cheerleader for Mary, my sister. She had this solid belief that Mary would eventually come around and become a believer. Grandmom had the belief that God was merciful and that He would bring Mary around, eventually. She had the faith of a mustard seed for

Mary. As for me, I'm not sure what Grandmom thought about me. She would ask if I met any "nice boys" lately or if I still went to the so-and-so church. Grandmom felt comfortable around me and we had a genuine love for each other. She was one special lady and had an opinion about everything, but only gave it if she was asked. I could tell that she was not worried about me. I dearly loved my Grandmom and cherished her opinions. She is my only living grandparent. My mom's parents died in a car accident years ago, and I have wondered, is that why she is such a worrier? My dad's father passed away when he was a young boy. His father went in for a gallbladder surgery and something went wrong. Grandmom does not really discuss it much. I think she still mourns her lost love.

Along with Thanksgiving and every big holiday, we would also have dinner together every Sunday. It usually took place sometime in the afternoon, either after Jeff's church service or late afternoon so that everyone could get ready for the next day's work. I really enjoyed our weekly family time together. It was an anchor in my life, not just a free meal, (unlike what my siblings thought it should be).

During dinner at Thanksgiving, I told my family about the accident I almost had at the bus stop and how I was saved by a strong and beautiful young lady. They all expressed how thankful they were that she was there to help me out. Yes, I agreed, but then I told them that I saw the same lady in Seattle. How strange is that! They all chewed their food in silence on that one.

"Stranger things have happened," expressed my father.

"Really? Like what?" I asked.

Dad didn't have an opinion on what those "other stranger things" were. "Honey, it's just an expression." Which began a discussion on strange things, like the Ripley's Believe It or Not Museum on the San Francisco pier, and the weird things they have inside the museum.

With the dinner moving into the dessert stage, Mary was serving Marionberry Cobbler with ice cream (she outdid herself this year). She then dropped the bomb that she met a nice guy named Damien. First all, Mary has had horrible luck with men. She just does not know how to pick them. There was this guy that was kind of homeless named Alan. She asked mom and dad if he could live at the house with them. That was a "no". Then there was this welder guy that would light his cigarettes with the flame torch. And how about the biker dude that would pick her up on his motorcycle and Mary always would wear a skirt! Yikes!

So, when Mary mentioned that she met a nice guy, there was a collective non-committable sound that was made. I had to turn my back so that I could do my eye roll. And of course, my mom asked the questions. Where did you meet him? Does he have a job? What makes him nice?

"I met him at a coffee shop on Sand Blvd", she related. "Yes, he does have a job but I not sure exactly what he does, and yes he is nice and can make intelligent conversation."

Cool, already a winner. Mom asked when we all could meet him.

"Mom, I just met him. I'm not ready for him to meet the parents." Mary closed that door pretty dang fast. I don't blame her. For her just to mention this Damien dude was a big deal. Let's see how long this one will last.

After dinner and cleanup, we all sat around the television and debated whether we were going to watch football or a movie. Every year it was the same discussion, and it would depend which team was playing. If it was the Seahawks, absolutely the TV was on for the game. We are big fans of our local within-the-state team. If it were another team that none of us liked, then it was a movie night. Either way, we all sank down into a turkey coma and fell asleep during the show. We would wake up during the closing credits with drool coming out of the corner of our mouths and say, "Gotta go."

I headed home, watching careful for any drunk drivers, and started preparing for the Black Friday sales the next day. I would stop at a gas station store and buy a newspaper for all the ads and plan out the attack for the next morning. The Friday sales started creeping in earlier and earlier and I was not willing to be the first in line unless it was for something special. Five or six in the morning was early enough for the free coffee and donuts and the mounds of socks for sale. This was an easy way to shop for the fam and it was better for my budget. I would put aside some money once a month throughout the year for this shopping day and for Christmas in general. I would also look for gifts for my co-workers and yes, even my boss. Even though my boss was rough to work with, he was a generous man at Christmas time. Last year he gave me a nice watch that I still wear and another year it was a nice necklace with a gold chain. I was pretty impressed and wondered if his wife shopped for the girls in his office. Another year, his wife was on an extended vacation (I think it was a separation) and we received bonus money instead. My boss was in a much better mood when his wife returned from her "vacation." Life in the office was a bit easier after that.

I have wracked my brain for what to get everyone this year. I was hoping that ideas would leap out from the pages of the newspaper that I was picking up from the 7-11 store. Usually, I can pick up on ideas from discussions made throughout the year of things to buy, but I have been so busy lately and not very intentional with my listening skills. I hate this kind of pressure that Christmas can put on me. The pressure of getting the right gift, the pressure of this kind of performance. Is this the year that everyone gets gift cards? Heaven forbid.

I got home and dumped my coat and purse in the chair next to the door. I put away my poke sack (my sack full of leftovers) in the refrigerator, and promptly settled down to scan the newspaper ads. I found some promising things that piqued my interest (for me that is) but not for anyone else. Isn't that the way of things? I thought of a juicer for Mary and for Jeff.....? Not sure what my parents would like. I wish I could afford airline tickets to somewhere but maybe a weekend at the coast would be nice. In fact, that was a great idea! It looks like I will be hitting the stores at about 5 in the morning for that juicer and having a good nap after that.

My alarm went off at 4:30 am and it was painful to get up. I am thankful that I will have the whole day off to lay around after my shopping. I did not get a particularly good night's sleep. My dreams were really weird;

I was chasing someone the whole night. I would just get close to that person to grab their coat and then they would disappear. I got up and brushed my teeth and hair and washed my face. I layered on my clothing for the different temperatures that I will experience while shopping. I planned on shopping at the large super stores so that meant that I needed to be ready for the crowds. And I do not want to forget my shopping list! I put wrapping paper and Christmas cards on my list late last night. And I want to pick up one more commemorative Christmas tree ornament that has the date on it.

The parking lot was packed full and I was driving up and down the lanes for a parking place. Over and over again. I was just about ready to say "forget it" when I saw someone walking to their car. Yes! I put my blinker on and sat and waited for them to pull out and into the spot I went. I got out of the car with my Black Friday fanny-pack around my waist and carried my own shopping bag into the store for the hunting extravaganza. The shopping carts can get in the way, unless you are buying big things. I am not getting big things this year so I do not need to be pushing that monster around. The fanny-pack works great and it keeps my hands free. As I enter the store, I can feel the excitement of the shoppers, hunting for the big deals of the day.

I stopped at the first center aisle and saw the large quantity of socks that are for sale. There are numerous large bins that are full of all kinds of socks that you could want. I got a few pairs for mom, crew socks for dad, dress socks for Jeff, and Mary will be receiving multi-colored wool socks. I also wanted some socks for myself. I have always decorated their Christmas gifts with socks or stuffed them with candy and treats. I have tried numerous ways to make them less unattractive. Then I'm off to the appliance section for the juicer. I thought of maybe hitting the auto section for Jeff's car. Geez, that is lame. Think, think! What else could I get him? Another tie? An automatic shoeshine buffer? As I was looking at the many juicer products and reading each box, out of the corner of my eye, I caught someone standing nearby. I shifted my body away from that person. I felt that they were too close for my comfort level. They will get the message to not intrude because of my body language, so I thought. But I could "feel" them watching me. Creepy.

I turned abruptly towards them and gruffly said, "Am I in your way?" It was the girl! From downtown and from Seattle and now she is here? What the....

"You!" She just stood there smiling as though she just pulled a prank. I thought of the only thing I could say, "I saw you in Seattle." She nodded her head in a yes. "You know this is really weird that I keep running into you." Again, she nodded her head yes. "Where are my manners? My name is Susie." I thrust my hand out to shake her hand and she took a small step backwards. She smiled and turned to walk away. "Wait! What is your name? I'm glad to meet you." I was trying desperately to keep the one-sided conversation going.

She turned back to me, cocked her head a bit and gave me a deep look, as though she was weighting her response. Finally, she said, "Angela." And walked away. Her voice sounded like a musical note. It was not too high and it was not low, like a radio show host. It was just right... wow, that sound like a nursery tale rhyme! I went to the end of the aisle where

Angela turned the corner to peek at her departure and she was nowhere in sight. Of course there were a lot of shoppers, but I didn't think she could disappear so quickly.

I finished my shopping in a fog. I felt satisfied with all my purchases, even the ornament of the baby Jesus, which is so unlike me. But what is Christmas without the nativity scene? The older I get, the more nostalgic I am getting. I read a bumper sticker recently that said, "Jesus is the reason for the season." That saying must have stuck with me. It is a true statement, but I have not taken much time to think about that kind of stuff lately. I have always left that up to Jeff. But it's not like I am a pagan or anything. I guess that I'm just kind of...neutral.

After my Christmas shopping spree, I usually go to a local coffee shop, which in this case happened to be in the store. I love Peets coffee and the aroma was calling my name. I ordered my usual, medium Latte, extra hot. I sat at one of the tables and contemplated about what had happened this morning. This is really weird. In fact, whenever I think of Angela, I think my interaction with her is bizarre. Angela is someone that I would love to get to know, but obviously she doesn't want the same thing. Do I have a sign on my forehead that says, "Loser, needs friends?"

The rest of the weekend was uneventful. I was looking forward to the Sunday family dinner. This time it was leftovers from Thanksgiving. Turkey something casserole, with green bean casserole and rolls with salad on the side. As we were all dishing up, Mary tilted her plate and bent down to sniff. "What is this mom? You've never made this before," in an indignant voice. My first thought was, why didn't Mary cook something for a change?

As usual, the conversation was all over the board. "Jeffrey, how was church today? What did you speak about?" "Mary, have you been seeing that guy from the coffee shop?" And then mom proceeded to tell us about a neighbor who fell in their driveway. After the conversation grinds down, I pipe up and said that I saw that girl again while shopping on Friday.

"Which girl?"

"The one I saw in Seattle. She was the one that saved me from falling."

"You fell in Seattle?" asked Mary. I rolled my eyes in exasperation. Mary needs to keep up with the conversation.

"No, when I almost fell getting on the bus after work," I replied.

"Where did you see her?"

"While shopping I said. Isn't it weird that I saw her again? Her name is Angela. I got that much out of her before she disappeared."

"She disappeared?"

"No silly. She just rounded the corner of the aisle I was in and I couldn't see her any longer."

"Which aisle were you in?" asked Mary.

"I'm not telling you since I was looking for something for you for Christmas. You are not getting that out of me smarty-pants!" We all chuckled.

Chapter Three

AS THE DAYS QUICKLY MOVED TOWARDS CHRISTMAS, THE busyness of the day fill to overflowing. The workdays became intense and the parties were many. There was the office party, then the neighborhood party, and Jeffrey's church bazaar and woman's tea. Also, there was the get together with girlfriends, as though we had not thought to get together at any other time of the year. It was hectic but also satisfying. I loved the activity, even though I may complain occasionally.

The attorney's office that I work in has many "specialty" lead attorneys with their lead egos. Then there are the paralegals, assistances, secretaries, and file clerks. I am a personal assistant to the lead corporate attorney, Mr. Mack, and my boss is all business. Mr. Mack can be an intense person and he can cut through any baloney that people can give out. He is perceptive and can tell when someone is being a bit shady or not telling the complete truth. Everyone wants his attention during this time of year. Most businesses are trying to tie up loose ends by the end of the year for their personal tax matters, which stem from their corporations. Or they are trying to "cut the deal" before the end of the year. Big business is happening! And also there is a lot of 'schmoozing' going on. Greasing the skids, fruit baskets are sent, cards were sent out thanking them for their business, and party invitations have been accepted.

As I walk to my bus stop after a long day, I am wondering what I am going to have for dinner since I forgot to go grocery shopping. I am carrying the desk lamp that I bought on sale on my lunch hour and because I missed my lunch, I am one hungry bear. I guess that is why I am thinking of food. I wonder if I have a breakfast bar in my purse.

I suddenly feel a tug on my sleeve and jerk my arm away. Who is touching me? I look up into Angela's face. Oh my gosh, it is her and she has a gorgeous man with her. She grabs my hand and starts pulling me down the street. When she grabbed my hand, electricity shot through my hand and up my arm. Wow, she gave me a shock!

"Angela, why are you pulling on me? And hello to you too," I say, as I try to pull my hand away. But her hand has a grip on me that will not let go. It would be nice to be introduced to this hunk of manhood with her but instead I was being propelled down the street for about a block and a half. We reach a dark alleyway with dumpsters against the wall in it. I could hear some scuffling noises in the alleyway next to one of the dumpsters and could barely see into the darkness. I could see a person wrestling with a woman, tugging at her purse. What the....?

There was a rage that surged through my stomach and up my throat when I realized what I was witnessing. Before I knew it, I went barreling into the alleyway and swung my desk lamp bag into the man that was standing over the woman. I hit him so hard that he fell over and tumbled into her. He jumps up and is holding a knife. My rage must have registered on my face and my defiance surged through my veins. Thank goodness, Angela and her friend were there with me. The man takes one look at me and runs off. I turn my attention to the woman, laying on the ground. This woman looks to be fairly young, in her late teens or early twenties. She is trying to adjust her clothing and making sniffling noises. I quickly sit down next to her and envelope her shaking form into my arms, holding her tightly, whispering words of comfort. I look around and there is no Angela or her friend. Geez! Where the heck did you go to? I am not sure if they went for help or what.

"Honey, are you hurt?" I asked the young woman. Her reply was negative, with a shake of her head, and her body began to shake just as violently as her negative reply.

"He tried to take my purse," she sobbed. I took out my phone and called 9-1-1 and explained where we were located. We just sat in the stinky alleyway, hugging her, and letting her know that she is safe with words of comfort. As we waited for the police to arrive, the alley smells wafted over us of old rotted food and acidic urine.

The police arrived and started taking down statements. The man did not complete his horrible intention but because the young lady was so traumatized, the police advised her to be checked out at the local hospital.

There are personnel there that will help her talk through this attack and check her to make sure that she is truly okay. After all, he did have a knife. I got her name and phone number because I wanted to stay in touch. She mumbled her thanks as she was led to the ambulance. I think she was in shock.

As I left the scene, I picked up my package with my now broken desk lamp. The box had been split open and the lamp was dangling from the package like a dead rabbit. Oh boy, I must have really walloped the guy. Good! The broken lamp was a small price to pay. I wonder what happened to Angela. She keeps disappearing. She is really a strange cookie. But I am thankful that I was there when the young woman needed help. Angela must have seen me down the street when she came upon that scene. But since she had that hunk with her why would she need me? I wonder if they were on a date? Maybe she just didn't want to get involved because she was with that guy. But why wouldn't the guy be chivalrous?

Boy, what a day! I was glad to be home and safe. That poor woman, holding onto her purse and being dragged into an alley. Downtown is becoming scarier and scarier. Thanks to Angela for propelling me in there to help, but then she disappeared. I have a few questions to ask her if I ever see Angela again. I guess as long as that girl is okay… I really walloped that guy! A chuckle escaped my lips.

Thoughts were swirling around in my head as I ran a bath. I usually take showers after my day at work, but tonight was definitely a bath night. I dumped some eucalyptus crystals in with some sweet-smelling lavender.

The combination can be intoxicating! I needed to de-crud my body of all the filth in the alley and relax. As I slunk down into the beautiful steaming warm water, I let a sigh of relief and contentment. There were more questions that were swirling around in my head than answers. However, I have given up on answering those questions. I just wanted to turn off my brain. But it wasn't working. My body was relaxing but my brain was not.

My phone rang as it was sitting on the toilet lid. I leaned over to read the caller ID. It was my friend Dawn. As I answered the call, Dawn babbled an apology about not going to Seattle with me. She wondered if I had time for a bite to eat tonight? There was a long pause. Do I want to go out or not? I knew that I would start talking about all the weird stuff that has happened from the last month or so. Do I really want to spill my guts? I declined her wonderful offer and asked for a rain check. How about after Christmas? I explained that I was in the bathtub trying to unwind from a hectic day. "No problem, girlfriend. I totally understand and we will reschedule for after Christmas. Maybe New Years. Do you have plans?"

"I haven't even thought that far in the future. Let's see what happens and that would be a great idea. Love you, Dawn and I'll call you next week to make a plan." We ended our call with pleasantries, and I sank back into the tub of now lukewarm water. I just didn't feel like being around anyone tonight, even if I love my girlfriend. She is a good friend, but she also usually wants to talk about herself. It would be a difficult night with her on a one-sided conversation, especially with all the stuff that has happened to me lately.

I got ready for bed, even though it was early in the evening. I watched some TV, with the word 'watch' as relative. I couldn't even tell you what was on. I had a fitful night's sleep, with dreams of running away or running to catch someone, or almost being caught. I seemed to wake up more tired than when I went to sleep.

I started getting ready for work and my stomach was rumbling. Did I eat last night? I don't believe I did! I fixed some scrambled eggs that I put on a piece of toast and wolfed it down. Then I grabbed my coat and was out the door. I got to the bus stop just as my bus was lumbering past. Darn! I missed the bus. I couldn't help but to stomp my foot in frustration. That means I will have to drive my car. The parking fee for downtown is outrageous and to even find a place on the street to park is worse than a nightmare. I will execute my backup plan, to drive to the carpark at the Max station. The Max is the light rail system in Portland. It works pretty well, is fast and efficient, and the people-watching is amazing. I do not like the Max because of the potential for car break-ins at the carpark and also it is not unusual to have some intimidation tactics by people on the Max itself. It is getting better with a security person walking the Max now and again. There are gang-like goons that come around and intimidate the commuters. Usually the goons are not there during the morning rush but depending on what time you leave work, they may be there.

I got a decent enough parking place at the carpark. It was under a light pole so that I will have lighting when I returned to my car. A girl needs to think of these things! Can you see that I am a planner? I hopped onto the next tram for downtown which means that I will get to work only 5 minutes late. Not bad for a messed-up morning. As usual the train was packed with nowhere to sit. I just had to stand and hang onto the upper rail bars. There was a shift in the crowd a few stops later, and I was able to get a seat. Just then, an elderly lady came on with her empty shopping bags flapping around her. I stood to give her the seat. Just then a kid popped into my seat. I turned a scowled at the impertinent scamp.

"I got up for this lady to take the seat. Please get out of my seat." He shook his head no. I looked around for his parent.

"Are you here by yourself?" He shook his head no.

Yelling out to the crowded train, "Hey, does this kid belong to anyone?"

Through the crowd came a young lady's voice. "I'm babysitting him, and we are going to the downtown park."

"That's real nice of you but he just took my seat that I was offering to this mature lady." The 'mature' lady was keenly observing all this hullabaloo with a mischievous smile on her face.

"Alex, get out of that seat. It is not yours. Where are your manners?" And he did not budge. "I'll tell your mom and dad all about this." And he promptly got up with a frown.

"Thank you so much Miss. You are a good babysitter," I said.

The elderly lady sat down and thanked me. I squatted down so that I was nose to nose with little Alex. "Do you know why we give our seats to the

Barbara Vogel

elderly?" He shook his head no. "Because it is all about respect for our elders. They are wiser than we are and have lived through tough things. Also, when they become elderly in years, they can be unsteady on their feet sometimes. We don't want this lovely lady to accidently fall when the train jerks, do we?" Alex shakes his head no.

"Alex, you are a good boy and I'll just take it that you didn't understand. You just learned some manners! Good for you! Your mom would be proud." Alex beamed at the compliment. I winked at the babysitter.

Before I knew it, it was time to get off the Max and trudge up the many blocks to my office building. The air smelled like snow was coming. Oh Lordy, I hope not. The days were getting colder and fall has come and gone. It is definitely winter season. Portland usually doesn't get snow until January or February. It always rains in December but in this cold weather it may begin to sleet or hail. It usually melts pretty fast but everyone freaks out when there is just a hint of snow coming. Portlanders do not know how to drive in the snow and Portland is situated around many hills, with downtown being in the valley. There are so many car accidents that happen! And the television news catches all the bad ones. A few years ago, the news station caught an out of control bus sliding sideways down a hill bouncing off the parked cars. It was brutal looking.

The young woman from last night was not far from my mind. I was always thinking about her. I hope she was okay. How could anyone just be okay after that? My head was down as I was walking through the crowds to my office building. I felt someone next to me, keeping pace with my

44

fast clip. I finally turned my head and recognized Angela. I stopped dead in my tracks. Forget about being on time for work!

"Hi Angela! Thanks for last night. I think that girl is gonna be alright. We came just in time. Did you see it happen? And by the way, where did you go afterwards? I could not find you. And who was that hunk you were with? Is that you boyfriend?" I vomited out questions as fast as I could, as though she would leave if I didn't talk fast enough. I was beginning to feel awkward after my questions trailed to a stop.

Angela just patiently stood there and smiled. I cleared my throat as to say, 'your turn to talk'.

Angela opened her perfectly formed mouth and said, "Good work." Her voice was like a singer's voice. It resonated through the air. It is hard to describe. I did not expect this voice of authority to come out of this petite woman. She turned to go. I yelled, "wait!" She turned back to me with a quizzical look on her face.

"Angela, I really want to get to know you. You keep showing up at the oddest places. Can I take you to coffee sometime and just talk?"

There was a short pause as though she was thinking it over. "You already know me and yes we can have coffee." And she turned to go.

"Wait…. When?" I asked.

"Soon," was the reply she gave over her shoulder.

People were trying to push past us on the sidewalk, and I was getting jostled. It was a quick exchange and before I knew it, someone had walked in between us. And she was already walking down the street and turning the corner. I felt thrilled that we were able to make a coffee date. Wait a minute! We didn't settle on a time or place. My short-lived thrill had now turned to frustration. Why the heck didn't I nail her down to a time? She is a slippery one and so evasive. This is so weird! I can't help but think of it as being really weird.

I went into work with a bounce in my step and a smile on my lips. Even though I had grief in my heart over the woman from yesterday, I was elated to finally connect with Angela. During lunch, I talked to the girls in the office about what had happened the previous day. I felt that I needed to warn my coworkers about the possibility of thieves and predators on the streets. I must admit, it felt good to talk about being a hero, kind of. Not exactly a hero. I truly believed that I was in the right place at the right time. And now that I really think about it, I was dragged to the right place at that precise time.

During my lunch break, I called the hospital where the girl was taken last night. I had lost her phone number and I wanted to check up on her. I talked to a triage nurse in the emergency room and she happened to be on duty the previous evening. She was insistent that she could not give out any information on the patient's identity or condition. I pretty much knew this since I work in an attorney's office, but I thought I would give it a try. And the nurse did not give a hoot that I worked in an attorney's office. That was probably more detrimental instead of being asset. It is not always good to pull out the attorney card. But the nurse actually made a mistake; she did mention that the patient had already been discharged. That was one piece of good news. The patient was not harmed enough to be kept overnight. Thank God. Now why did I think that? I haven't thanked God for a long time. I really should do that more.

I would not call myself religious. But I do have faith in God. I do go to church once in a while and I do have a brother that is a pastor, even though that relationship shouldn't be a "get out of jail free" card that I can play in front of Saint Peter at the pearly gates. My mother was raised Catholic so a lot of my belief systems may have come from my upbringing. She prayed to the saints and would take me to Mass when I was a young girl. The quietness and solemnest of the church had an impact on me. I remember dipping my fingertips into the holy water, kneeling, standing, and then kneeling again during Mass. But we stopped going before my Confirmation into Catholicism. I don't know why we stopped going but we did. I know my dad never went with us. I think after that my parents went to different churches. My dad called it, "shopping for a church." We eventually landed in a non-denominational church that my father liked. He appreciated the pastor and his "fiery sermon." I liked Pastor Smith too. He had a passion in him that burned bright. When he preached, his face would light up. I remember a sermon he gave that really impacted me. It was about the Jesus he knew as a fun God, that He was hilarious. I never thought of Jesus as being fun. I always imagine Him as walking around with His hands in a prayerful posture and being peaceful enough to hold a lamb in His arms.

When I got home that evening, I couldn't wait to call Grandmom and tell her about what happened the previous day. She was so thrilled that I was able to help that young woman. She admonished me to be careful as I walk the downtown streets. "That could have happened to you." Grandmom did the caring and lovingly scold that I knew she would do. I knew she worried about me working downtown and she had expressed her opinions about this but she knew that it couldn't be helped. Grandmom asked me some questions about Angela that I could not really answer. These were questions that I was already asking in my head about her.

"Grand, I will let you know if there is any more information about Angela when I have coffee with her. And no, I don't know when that will happen, but I'll let you know." I signed off the call with love. I really do love my Grandmom. She is one special lady.

The next call was to my mom. I took a deep breath as I dialed the familiar number. I love my mother, but her questions are a little bit more on the naggy side of things. I wish she would be just proud of me. I feel like she examines me instead of just loving me. This may be totally my imagination, but I feel like she treats me differently than she does Mary. She raises me into a higher expectation than she does Mary. Mom makes excuses for Mary and her behavior but for me, there are no excuses. I know this sounds harsh and I really need to examine my own thoughts on this. Where in my childhood did this come from?

My mother was aghast at the whole story. She couldn't believe there was an attack in broad daylight. She was so relieved that the young girl was okay. That brought on a new conversation of whether I should be working downtown at all.

"Where else would I work, mom? I have been working there for years and I am doing great and I am happy there. It was just fortunate that I was pulled into that situation in the alley."

"Susie, who is this Angela? Is she a new friend or does she work in your office? Isn't she the one that helped you when you started to fall a while ago?"

"Yep mom, she is the one. I asked her to coffee, but we haven't settled on a date for that yet."

"Well Susie, I want to meet her someday." I thought, so would I! I wondered when or if that would ever happen.

"Good night mom. I'll see you on Sunday for lunch. What do you want me to bring?" We said our goodbyes.

Chapter Four

CHRISTMAS WAS RAPIDLY APPROACHING AND SO WAS OUR office Christmas party. Our office really looked forward to this party every year. Besides getting a Christmas bonus from the partners in the firm, it was great to celebrate the holidays with my coworkers. I loved getting dressed up and going fancy. The firm usually had their party at a nice hotel with large banquet rooms or a nice restaurant. The other great thing, we are able to meet our coworker's spouses or significant other. I usually did not invite a guest to these occasions since I did not like all the gossip that swirled amidst their quizzical looks. But I loved to watch all the other attendees. I liked to see who was getting along with their spouse, or not, who drank too much, whose outfit was not really appropriate, and who's outfit was elegant and tasteful. It was just a wonderful spectacle to observe. I think I would classify myself as a 'watcher' and that is my very favorite thing to do. I loved to observe, and to figure out what the motivations are behind their behaviors. I watch mannerisms, intentions, body language, and the way people express themselves. I guess that is why I am so successful in doing my job well. If people-watching was a sport, then I would be in the Olympics. I people watch on the bus, at my work, as I shop and as I walk in my neighborhood. I would say that I am a professional observer! I should put that on my resume.

I had not bought a new outfit for the party and I only had a few days to do so. I don't know where the time has gone! I need to decide when to go shopping and where. Do I shop downtown or at the mall? Do I have any ideas of what I want to wear? A skirt and fancy top, or a dress? Long or short? What color? That could be a whole new pitfall. As usual, I began to ask my girlfriends at the office what they were planning to wear. I received a variety of answers without any help about my own personal fashion. The Christmas outfits were usually a black dress or something red, but I want to wear something different and spectacular. One of the partners usually has his family attend and he has this gorgeous son that is about my age. I wonder if he will be here this time? I sincerely hope so.

I decided to head to the mall after work tonight. I would just take the number 78 bus to the large mall on the side of town where I live and I hoped that I get off work on time. I can just eat at the food court at the mall and not have to worry about dinner. They have great food choices there, depending on what I feel like at the time. And at the mall, they have tons of dress shops, including the big department stores. I am hoping that the dress I find will not be too expensive so that I can buy a pair of shoes to go with it. Maybe a great black skirt so that I can wear it to work also. But I wanted something spectacular. The indecisions of an outfit buying were already beginning to play out in my head. I want to be strategic about what I am going to buy. I should have done this on Black Friday during the awesome sales. Why didn't I? Oh yeah…. I got side-tracked when I saw Angela. I may need to wait for the after Christmas sales to shop for the rest of my clothes. Today, I will be hunting for the one dress. The one spectacular dress. The one that will make heads turn. Yeah, right! Not. I will need a whole makeover for that!

In each one of the shops, I would go to the sale rack first. I was not finding anything that really stuck out. I was beginning to get frustrated. I was milling around a shop with dresses hanging off my arm when I overheard a couple of girls talking by the dressing room. I could hear bits and pieces of their conversation. What caught my attention was the words "don't get caught" and "hide it." The red alert was ringing in my ears. I hate dishonesty. I guess it is the trained 'legal' side of me. As the girls emerged from the dressing room, I stepped in front of them. They came up short and their eyes challenged me with a stare. I gave them my business card that I had dug out of my purse. "Here is my card for the attorney firm that I work for. It is for when you get caught today. But my firm is not cheap," I said with a slight smile. One of girls hesitated but the other was defiant. I looked at the hesitant one, "It's not worth it." And turned around to go. I was not interested in the dresses that were over my arm, so I hung them up on the rack and proceeded to leave. I could see out of the corner of my eye that the one girl who was hesitant went back into the dressing room. I presumed that she was dumping off the stuff she was taking. I pray that it was so.

I went into the neighboring dress shop and came across a gorgeous gray dress. It was perfect! Where have you been all my life? It was long with a high waist that settled underneath the bosom. The neckline swooped down to an off the shoulder sexy ¾ sleeved length with a white cuff. The skirt of the dress had a slit up the side to approximately halfway up the thigh. The fabric felt scrumptious and graceful, had a slight shimmer and it held its form as you moved. The dress was snug from the bodice until the slit and then billowed out slightly for greater depth. It is so thrilling when you know you have got the perfect dress immediately as you slide into it. Even the salesgirls were impressed as I exited the dressing room to swish around the store. Sold!

As I exited the shop with my dress packaged and hanging over my arm, I noticed a commotion in the mall. As I craned my neck to see what was happening, I saw a familiar coat on a girl that was kneeling on the ground, a policeman towering over her. Oh geez, it was the girls from the previous shop. They must have been caught shoplifting. As I moved closer, I saw the one girl with tears streaming down her cheeks while the other sat with her head down and hands behind her back. The tear-streaked teen was intently listening to the officer explain that he was going to call her parents and have them pick her up, since she did not have any merchandise on herself. Then the officer took a breath and turned to the other teen and proceeded to tell her that she was going downtown with him to be booked. As I passed by, the crying teen caught my look and stared. I saw a slight node of her head as though to say thank you. And I nodded back. Whoa, how sad. And how did I know that they were going to get caught? I guess the odds were in my favor.

There are times in our life where we reach a crossroad. One path leads one direction, and another path leads to another. Each person

inherently knows the difference between the two paths, but peer pressure or life's circumstances make one path look easier than the other or
at least 'decorated' better. For example, the Hollywood crowd. There
is a crossroad that one can take that leads to drugs, indiscretions for
movie parts, dishonesty to pad the resume, the run for money, yada,
yada. It is difficult to be honest and going against the grain in the en-
tertainment industry, especially when it may cost you something you
want. I know because we, at the attorney firm, represent some clients
from that industry. Their obscure view of where the line of integrity is
gets blurred, to the point of getting themselves into trouble, hence the
attorney calls. I suppose this includes our clients in large corporations
that are ladder-climbing to the top rung. There is a point where you
make a decision to go onto a path that begins a slippery downward
cycle. And it is hard to notice this slippery path because you think
you are doing the right thing, at the moment. I know that I have had to
make that decision at the office. I have become my boss's conscience
at times when he has wanted to fudge a little. My boss is a pretty honest guy, but he is also ruthless and wants to win in order to get the best
for his client. We have had heated discussions but ultimately, he is my
boss. I also know he trusts me.

All this was running through my head as I went into a discount shoe
store. I wanted to see if I could find gray shoes or at least ones that
could look great with this amazing dress. I found a pair of see-through
strapped, block-heeled shoes. The strap over the toes and distal foot was
a clear color, while the upper strap around the ankle was black. The long
dress would hide the upper strap and block heel. I have had a pair of
stilettos get caught in the hem of a long dress before and I almost ended

up headfirst in a fountain. It is hard to be graceful after making a scene like that. I am learning from my mistakes.

As I am exiting the store with my new purchase, I hear a yell from down the mall. "Stop, thief." As I turned my head to look, a guy came barreling into me. It took my breath away and I observed the scenario as though in slow-motion, with this guy falling to the ground. Within seconds, another guy was on top of him wrestling with him. I glued myself to the wall so that I could stay away from this WWF wresting match. And then there was a moment of silence, but only a slight moment before a screaming lady came upon the pair. The guy on the bottom of the dogpile was the purse snatcher, and the top dog was the rescuer-son of the screaming lady and following was the overweight and breathless security guard. The purse snatcher was subdued, and the angry son was holding back his indignant rage, and the guard was just daring the snatcher to move so that he could use his new taser-gun. As the crowd gathered to watch the show, the lady came over to me and thanked me for stopping this thug. She kept saying how amazing it was for me to stop him. "Ma'am, I didn't do a thing. I just happened to be coming out of the store." She insisted that she saw me stick out my foot to trip the perpetrator. The police arrived, for the second time that night. They took statements and handcuffed the thug. The lady and son thanked me profusely and was glad that I was willing to help. The guard was relieved it was over.

As the guard was leaving, he off-handedly said, "I'm sure glad this was all on video." I grabbed his arm, ever so gently, and said, "Is it possible that I can see that? The lady kept saying that I stuck out my foot and I remember it differently that this guy ran into me. I sure would like to see what happened, since it was so quick." The guard turned out to be a nice guy and chatted as we went up the main security office. After he was 'keyed' into the office, he asked the other security guy to replay the recording of the purse snatching. "Yeah, I have it right here. I knew you would be by to watch it. Besides, we have to save it in case the police need it for evidence."

The tape was readied for replay and the guard hit 'play.' The security camera was amazingly placed just opposite the shoe store. I could see the shoppers passing by as they window shopped. I could see plainly myself exiting the store and see my head swivel for something that was about to happen. There was no sound on the video, but I could hear plainly in my head the shout of 'stop.' What happened next was shocking. I saw myself being accelerated back towards the wall so much so that my feet stuck out. Wait...what? "Sir, could you play that back in slow motion?" As the slow motion began to click by, I saw my head turn again, and then myself being moved backwards. "Sorry sir, one more time again please, in slow motion." My head turns, and... "Stop!" The guard hits the stop button. As I leaned forward to almost put my nose on the screen, I see an imprint of a compression on my chest. I see my clothes flatten against my skin as the other part of my clothes are swishing in the opposite motion. As I stare into the screen, I can feel the guards face next to mine. He asked, "Who is pushing you back? No wonder your legs are sticking out." My mouth is hanging open as we look at each other. As I gather myself together, I thank him for letting me see the video and try to make a fast exit.

As I walk numbly to the exit doors of the mall, I realize how late it had become. I did not want to take the bus home at this late hour and must walk through the neighborhood in the dark. I called for an Uber and it happened to be only minutes away. They probably figured that the shoppers would be calling since it was closing time for the mall.

The Uber driver and I rode in silence. My thoughts were a million miles away and before I knew it, we were in front of my residence. I gave him a healthy tip and asked for him to wait until I unlocked the outer door to my building. Once inside my apartment, I kicked off my shoes, and hung up my new dress, which had some wrinkles from the push against the wall incident. I put on some water to boil for a cup of Chamomile tea. What a day! I need to wind down from all the excitement.

I awoke with a start, with a stiff neck. I realized that I had fallen asleep in the chair, again, with a half cup of cold tea sitting on the end-table next to me. I reached up and wiped off a small amount of drool that was sitting in the corner of my mouth. Oh my, what time is it? I glanced over into the kitchen to see what the clock said. Three o'clock in the morning. I was having difficulty working out the kinks of stiff muscles as I was navigating, turning off the house lights and going to the bedroom. I suddenly saw a shadow of movement out of the corner of my eye. My head swiveled to the far corner of the room. It was dark in that corner, and I saw a small shadow of something dart behind a chair. Daggumm it! It had better not be a mouse. I quickly switched the lights on and ran over to the chair, pushing it away from the corner. I had realized that I had grabbed one of my shoes that were laying by the door and I was ready to pounce. Nothing was there. I turned the chair over. Nothing. Was I imagining things? No! I definitely saw something. And now I was creeped out. How am I gonna sleep now?

I finally fell asleep after a couple of hours, just in time to wake up groggy. This is going to be a long day. I made a note in my phone to pick up some mouse traps on my way home tonight. I put a reminder that I needed to make an appointment for a pedicure on Saturday morning. I needed perfect toes to show off in my new heels. I barely made the bus, and I was thankful for the mindless ride. I was having difficulty getting rid of my foggy mind, especially since I needed to be sharp today. We were expecting a big client, a CEO of a large corporation, to come in today about business issues he was having. His secretary called early this morning to schedule a longer meeting about another 'personal matter', which usually means a possible divorce. Depending on the problem, we have attorneys that specialize in different areas. We have a family law, corporate attorneys, tax attorneys, and criminal law attorneys. My boss pretty much has his fingers in all the pies and can delegate to the appropriate attorneys and at least confer with them.

As soon as I stepped into the office, I grabbed two coffees, a pad, and a pen, and head to the boss's private office. As usual, he was already there. "Good morning Mr. Mack." Mr. Mack isn't much on small talk and begins to rattle off the instructions for the day. Mr. Peterson, the CEO, was arriving at two this afternoon and we had things to prepare. And so my day begins. My fogginess began to dissipate and my brain kicks into gear, full steam ahead. Mr. Mack informed me that the client called early this morning with a new problem. Along with the other problems, he was bringing us a potential new problem that needed to be squelched if it arises. That sounded intriguing and definitely sounded like a divorce.

As 1:30 in the afternoon rolled around, I finally pulled into the kitchen to heat up a quick-frozen meal. I needed to get something in my tummy before the client arrived. I knew that once he arrived, there was no time for food. As I was taking my second bite of ravioli, the receptionist came barreling in. The client, Mr. Peterson, had arrived early. Grrrrr. "No problem," I said, with a plastic smile on my face. I told her to inform Mr. Mack of the early arrival and ask if he was available. "I will come right away to bring the gentleman to the conference room," I assured her. As the receptionist was leaving, she tossed out the comment that the client had his daughter with him. What? I wasn't going to babysit a kid!

As I wiped my mouth, smoothed a quick lipstick over my lips, and shook out the crumps from my skirt, I walked to the front of the office, all in one quick and practiced motion. With a smile on my lips and my outstretched hand to Mr. Peterson, I introduced myself. He had stopped pacing the foyer and I could tell that he was agitated but trying to hide it. He shook my hand formidably and turned to introduce his daughter. I stood there shocked! Well, well, if it isn't the girl from last night at the mall. She was just as shocked but clearly had difficulty hiding it. She mumbled her hello. Her father was quick to pick up the exchange between us. He turned to his daughter and asked if she knew me.

"Yes.... No.... I mean, I saw her last night at the mall. I never met her. She is the one I told you about."

"The girl you were with?" with his eyes narrowing.

"No Dad." She said with an eye roll. "She is the one that said it wasn't worth it."

Mr. Peterson gave me a discerning and appreciative look. I could tell that I had just gone up several pegs on his ladder of gratitude. He owed me one and he knew it. Not that I would ever cash in on it. I was curious how he would take this. He appeared to me like a man that didn't like to owe anyone. I gave him a slight smile of pretended humbleness, and a shrug of my shoulders, hoping to disarm him with the silent communication that he did not owe me anything. He gave me a node. The point was made.

The pair, along with his personal assistant, followed me to the conference room. With his daughter there, obviously we were going to take care of her situation first before delving into his other concerns. Mr. Mack was surprised to hear about the whole mall thing. Mr. Big Wig talked, then his daughter, then myself, all the while Mack was making quick notes.

"What is your concern with your daughter?" asked Mr. Mack. The corporate CEO stated that his concern was about the unwise and unwanted media attention. He was investing and possibly wanting to buy the mall and this incident was not the best timing. As I sat there, I thought, when is this 'incident' ever good timing? His daughter, whose name was Kelly, was sitting there eating humble pie. I could tell that she wished to become invisible. This was a great lesson of the consequences for her actions. I am so thankful that was not worse.

Mr. Mack was quick to tell the CEO that the media could be handled promptly, since Kelly was an 'innocent' party to all this. She was not booked, and she was let go by the police. The relief in the conference room was palpable. Kelly let out a big sigh. Mr. Mack turned to Kelly and looked her in the eye. "You know that you missed a bullet there, don't you? You should be thankful that you took Susie's recommendation and put the merchandise back. You should be incredibly careful who you hang out with. People like your so-called friend, can use you and bring you into situations that are hard to get out of. Plus, you gave your dad some stress that he didn't need. He loves you and wants the best for you. Do you understand, Kelly?" Kelly nodded her head. She looked towards her dad with tears in her eyes.

"Dad, like I said before, I am really sorry." Mr. Peterson grabbed his beautiful daughter and gave her a big hug. His voice was croaky as he indicated that he needed to move into new business. This large muscular CEO was not used to signs of affection to his precious daughter and the croaky voice brought a smile to Kelly's face. There was a knock on the conference door. The receptionist, with a blush, was interrupting. No one ever interrupts in the conference room! She was apologizing profusely but looking to me said that there was a news media person there. The relief feeling just got sucked out of the air. The agitation in the room was heavy. Mr. Mack started to rise. "Let me take care of this. I don't understand how they found out you were here," indicating to the CEO.

The receptionist interrupted Mr. Mack. "Sir, they want to see Susie here. Apparently, she is a hero, and they want to ask her some questions." All head swiveled towards me. I sat there with my jaw hanging open. The receptionist went on to say, "I guess Susie, you stopped a purse snatcher last night. The lady who was robbed, her son is one of the producers of the news station."

"Oh no!" My hands flew up to cover my face in shock. "How in the world did they find me?" The receptionist said that there was a business card left at the scene. My eyes flew to Kelly, who's face registered surprise. Our business cards have a small thumbnail picture on the card. The guard must have recognized the card as mine.

"Mr. Mack, let me go take care of this. I apologize. I will be right back." Mr. Mack had a slight proud grin on his face. He knew that this was mortifying to me and he was enjoying seeing me squirm. As I quickly walked to the front foyer, I was trying to formulate what to say to the newsperson. I apologized for their inconvenience, but that they needed to make an appointment, and I have no comment and I am thankful that the lady had her purse returned. I was just being a good citizen. This took all of a few moments and I was heading back into the conference room. I realized that I was perspiring for the first time in a year. Usually nothing rattles me, well almost nothing.

Mr. Mack indicated that he had business to discuss and suggested that I take Kelly for a coffee or hot chocolate. Obviously, I did not need to be present to take notes and privacy was more important. I was relieved and happy to oblige. I indicated that we would walk down to the local coffee shop and to give me a call when they were done. Mack nodded his head in assent and went right back to looking at some documents.

Kelly and I grabbed our coats, I talked to the receptionist to let her know we were going to the coffee shop, and off we went. It was great to be out of the office. We sloshed through the wet sidewalk, making small talk until we put our order in and sat at a table next to the window. Kelly was sincere in her gratitude for last night. I asked her how she knew the other girl. She was from her school. "Don't you go to a private school?" Kelly nodded her head yes. She explained that the girl comes from a divorced household and her parents are never around.

"That is too bad. I have been fortunate to have parents that are still married, and I go to their house every Sunday for lunch or dinner. My brother and sister go too. We all meet as a family." I said. This seemed to surprise Kelly.

"You don't hang out with your parents?" I asked.

"No not much. Dad seems pretty busy. When he is at home, he is usually on the phone and taking care of business. But he tries to stay connected. We go on vacations and stuff. I don't have a mom. She passed away when I was much younger, and I seem to be losing the memory of her. I mean, like her perfume smell and how she cooked breakfast and made my lunches. I still remember, but it is fading. I have her picture in my bedroom and that helps." Kelly suddenly appeared to be uncomfortable. "I don't know why I'm telling you all this."

"No worries," I said. "People open up to me all the time. I think it is because they know that I will keep their confidences, and I do." Kelly seemed to relax.

"Well, I know your Dad loves you, otherwise he wouldn't be so anxious for you. You threw him a curve ball and he is not sure how to handle it. You are his daughter, not just someone who works for him. You are his only precious daughter and I think he is still trying to figure out how to raise you." I said.

"That's the truth." Kelly said with a chuckle. There was a moment of silence as Kelly processed our conversation.

"Your Dad is realizing that you are growing up and becoming a woman, and you are not a kid any longer. So, my advice is, don't act like a kid and do dumb stuff. Act like the woman that you want to become." We sat there in silence as the words soaked into Kelly's mind. "What kind of woman do you want to become?"

"No one has ever asked me this before. I know you are not asking what I want to do in life but what I want to become. That's a much deeper question." Kelly muttered. "It's a really great question. I need to think about that." After a pregnant pause, Kelly added, "I think I would like to be like my mom. She was kind and dedicated to my Dad and me. She loved to laugh and have fun. She loved to read me stories at bedtime. My Dad and I really miss her."

"It sounds like you remember your mom pretty well, and I sense that you will be just like her. I can see that you have a kind heart. Otherwise you wouldn't have wanted to hang out with that girl from school. I have a sense that you were just trying to be nice to her. But instead you got pulled into something that could have been really bad. I am so thankful that your sense of honesty had won out and you returned that merchandise. Please do not stop being kind to people. Just be careful not to cross a line."

"That's the truth. I think I have learned a lesson," Kelly sighed.

"And that is the best news I have heard all day!" I said with a laugh. And we both shared a giggle.

I felt the tension leave Kelly as relief set in. We seemed to be starting a friendship. I really liked this kid. She had a good head on her shoulders. As I was looking out the window at the people rushing past on the way to their destinations, I saw Angela standing on the sidewalk just past the window.

"Kelly, I see a person that I need to talk to. Could you give me a second and I'll be right back?" Kelly nodded her head in consent.

I jumped up out of my seat and pushed past the people standing in line for their coffee. Out the door I went, lickity split, with a huge grin on my face.

"Hi Angela. It is nice to see you here. I was wondering if I could get your phone number," I asked.

"Sorry but I don't have a phone." Angela said. My face must have shown my surprise and disappointment. This development really rattled me. Who doesn't have a phone? How can you function? I could tell Angela was enjoying my discomfort in this new knowledge.

"How am I ever going to meet you again? I do want to get together with you sometime. You seem like an interesting person to get to know. And I do want to get to know you." I was surprised at my forthrightness. Angela grinned at this.

"No worries. How about in a couple of days? I meet you here for a coffee."

"Great!" I replied. Angela turned to leave. "Wait. What time?" I asked in a rush.

"You pick." Angela shrugged.

"How about this time." I suggested, even though I had no idea what time it was. It was the first thing that popped into my mind. Angela indicated a yes with a nod and strolled off with a wave of her hand. As I turned to go back into the coffee shop, I realized a huge mistake. 'In a couple of days?' What day was that? Oh no! A couple means two, right? Oh crap, this is bad. Today is Thursday and a couple of days will be Saturday, the day of the party. I checked my phone for the time. It was late afternoon. Just when I wanted to be getting ready for the party. Priorities. What are my priorities? With a definite determination, I knew that this was a priority, to meet with Angela. I can always use the office to change into my dress. I will improvise and it will work out.

I headed back into the coffee shop and to the table where Kelly was sitting. "I'm sorry about that. It was a total fluke that I saw a friend on the sidewalk, and I needed to catch her." Kelly gave me a strange look.

"Are you okay?" I asked Kelly, wondering what that look was all about.

Kelly asked, "who were you talking to?"

"Her name is Angela," I mentioned, as I stirred my Cappuccino.

Kelly just stared at me for a bit. "I didn't see that you were talking to any lady."

I knotted my eyebrows with a quizzical look. "What do you mean? Angela was standing on the sidewalk," I said with a toss of my hair.

"Susie," with a long pause. "There was no one there. You were not talking to anyone that I could see. I was watching you." Kelly and I just stared at each other in disbelief. I was having a hard time believing her and she was just as confused as I was.

Finally, I asked, "what do you mean no one was there?"

Kelly said, "Susie, you were talking to the air."

Chapter Five

"KELLY, PLEASE DO NOT MENTION THIS TO YOUR DAD. I AM not nuts. And I have to figure this out." Kelly politely said she would not tell her dad about the non-person person. This was really, really weird. I could tell that Kelly just thought I was peculiar, and I could also tell that she was inwardly glad to keep this secret. Her dad's attorney-assistant was a nut job. Secrets like this can come out at the most opportune time, when she needed it.

Kelly's father seemed relieved and satisfied when his meeting ended with Mr. Mack. He thanked me profusely for taking Kelly out for a coffee. And Mr. Mack said later that the meeting was successful, and they achieved some good headway. Kelly and I seemed to have bonded and I really like her. Everyone seemed to be in good mood as they parted, except for me. I was not in a good mood! I was in a disturbed, confused, and unsettled mood. I am a logical person. I am analytical. There are no such thing as invisible people. Kelly must have been mistaken. Angela was real when I was speaking with her.

The rest of the afternoon flew by and I began to relax on the bus ride home. While I was on the bus, I started a Google search for "unseen." My search gave me some interesting things. I found a movie reference that looked scary and a reference to psychiatric symptoms. Yikes. Then I came upon a statement that said: "The phrase "seeing the unseen" does carry some context, though it evokes the idea of the supernatural, and being able to "see" things which are outside of human perception…to discover; perceive; detect." Hum, this sounded interesting. As I look up and out of the window to think about this, I just realized I missed my bus stop. I signaled for the bus to stop at the next stop and realize I now must walk 8 blocks to my house. Dang.

The evening was a blur and so was the next day as I pondered about this notion of the unseen and supernatural. There must be a logical explanation about all this. I bet that Angela was just beyond Kelly's eyesight, or hidden against the wall and Kelly could not see her. That is the only clarification that I will accept right now.

Saturday rolled around and as I got up to make a cup of coffee, I realized I had not made the appointment for a pedicure. I started phoning around but most of the shops were full. I knew that I had to do a "walk in" appointment and wait in line. I was frustrated at my forgetfulness. Mr. Mack was kind enough to grant me permission to change at the office, as long as I would reset the alarm. I cleaned my apartment, which was my Saturday ritual, and I jumped into the shower. After I was scrubbed clean, I made up a bag to bring with me so that I could get ready downtown. It included a brush, hair pins in case I want to do an updo, makeup bag, my new shoes, and jewelry in case I want to wear it. I looked around my bedroom to see if there was anything else I missed. Looks like I got everything. I left the building and realized that I forgot my dress. Where is my head?

I found a nail shop that only had a half hour wait. I remembered to bring flip flops for after the pedicure. Which is hilarious to wear sandals in December. I love pedicures, they are so relaxing. I tried to numb my brain with a celebrity style gossip magazine. I can't tell you what I read because my mind was not on any of the articles. It was constantly drifting to the afternoon meeting with Angela. I am hoping to pin her down with some questions that she always seems to avoid.

I drove downtown and went into the office parking garage. On the weekends I did not have to worry about where to park since it was pretty much empty. I was still an hour early for my meeting with Angela. I went up to the office and deposited my dress and bag, set the office alarm, and then took the elevator to the lobby. There were the food trailers about 3 blocks away and just thinking of them made my tummy rumble. I realize that I had not eaten today.

I love the food carts. They have the best international foods, ever! They are legendary and quite popular in this area. The Korean tacos and Asian-fusion rice bowls are to die for, along with the Thai and Indian food. Today, I do not want anything too spicy, since my stomach is doing flip flops for the meeting that was about to happen and for tonight's fun party. I settled on 2 fish tacos and a water. There was a chill in the air, and I had to eat outside, so I wasn't wasting any time over my scrumptious meal. I gobbled the delicious lunch right down.

Then I was off to the coffee shop. I was a little early, but at least I was going to be sitting inside in the warmth. I ordered my Americano and got a nod from the barista who recognized me. She mentioned that she had never seen me here on a Saturday, as we made small talk.

I found a table by the window that a couple were just vacating. I sat and sipped. I checked the time on my phone and only had a 15-minute wait. As I looked up, Angela was already sitting opposite me.

"Oh, I didn't hear you arrive. Can I buy you a coffee or anything?"

Angela shook her head in decline. "No thank you."

"Thanks for meeting me here. I have so many questions and I just wanted to talk. It is really strange that I see you in the most bizarre places, even in Seattle." Angela just sat there smiling and looking at me. I was beginning to feel uneasy under the scrutiny. And I gave a nervous chuckle to break the ice. And then silence. She didn't say anything and neither did I. But that did not seem to bother her.

I finally cleared my throat and said, "So what do you do for a living?" At this Angela threw her head back and gave an uproarious laugh. "What do you mean 'for a living'?" Angela said.

"I mean, what do you do for work, for a job?" I asked.

"I don't have a job, I work for my Father." Angela announced.

"Well that must be nice. What does he do?"

"He takes care of everything. I help him." I am realizing that Angela is not big on talking. Her sentences are short and clipped. And not much information. This is gonna take some work on my part, I am realizing.

"Don't you find it kind of strange that we keep running into each other, Angela? It must be fate." I said.

"It is not fate," Angela gave a thin-lipped reply.

"Then what do you think it is if it is not fate?" I inquired.

"It is providence." Providence? What is she talking about? What the heck is providence? Like provision?

"No, it is Godly protection for this moment." I did a double take. Did Angela just answer my question that I did not ask out loud?

"So....." I just trailed off my sentence. I was trying to grasp my thoughts that were flying around like feathers during a pillow fight.

"Are you saying that God protects me?" I asked.

"Of course." She answered matter-of-factly. "And so do I."

I sat there staring at her. What? Did I hear her correctly? "What exactly do you mean Angela?"

"I protect you. I help you." I sat back in my chair. Sudden memories of my almost falling in the street came streaming into my mind. Or how about the time that I fell off my bike in front of a car and the car narrowly missed me.

"You must be like a guardian angel," I laughingly said.

"Exactly, you are correct."

"What?" I shouted.

"Shhhhh" said Angela. She started giggling. "You know, people don't see or hear me." I started looking around the coffee shop. People were staring at me or trying to avoid looking but still peeking. There was an uncomfortable silence in the whole shop. I quickly looked down into my half-drunk Americano coffee cup. Oh gosh, this is not happening. I have gone off my rocker. Is this really happening? Is this for real?

Angela said, "Let's go for a walk." I quickly jumped up to follow her out of the shop.

"I don't understand any of this Angela. Please explain it to me." I was desperately trying to get back into my logical mind. "Are you really an angel?"

"Yes I am. God loves you so much that He sent me to be with you and to protect you. That doesn't mean that absolutely nothing happens to you, but I am able to help you with the enemy."

"Why am I just discovering being able to see you? Did you just start coming around?"

"No, I have been with you even before you were born."

"So why can I finally see you now?"

"I think that is a question that you should ask the Almighty."

"Can you ask Him for me?"

"No. He wants to hear from you."

"You mean I just ask Him? Does He hear me all the time? What if I don't hear from Him?"

"Then ask again."

"Gotta go. And besides you need to get ready for your party," Angela reminding me.

"How do you know about my party?"

"Susie, I know everything about you. Chow." Instead of Angela walking off, she simply was gone. I found myself standing in the middle of the sidewalk, alone. An angel? Really? I must have stood there for some time trying to wrap my head around everything. I finally awoke from my stupor when a homeless man asked for money. I fished into my coat pocket and found a dollar.

"God bless," the homeless man said.

I rushed back to the office. I started up one of the computers and googled "angels." The first thing that came up was the Los Angeles Angels. Oh geez. Finally, after searching for the right definition, I read that angels were intermediaries between God and humanity. I knew there were angels in the Bible, and I had heard of them in Sunday school but I really did not give it much thought. I checked the time on my phone and realized that I needed to stop what I was doing and start getting ready. I shifted into glamour mode. I wanted to look nice for this Christmas party.

The party was all the way into the neighboring city of Vancouver. It would take 20 to 30 minutes to get there from downtown Portland, so I needed to get my butt into gear. It was in a grand hotel that had a western log style motif. The Heathman Lodge has great food and it is always beautifully decorated for the holidays. It was a nice pick for this year's festivities.

I parked my car close to the entrance and came sauntering in with a shawl over my bare shoulders. I felt pleased with how my outfit and makeup had turned out. I checked the directory in the front foyer for the correct banquet room and headed down the hallway. I could hear music and the buzz of conversation as I came near the doorway. Mr. Mack had stationed himself at the entrance, so that he could be the official greeter. He shook my hand pleasantly and gave me a fatherly compliment on my appearance. That meant a lot to me since I knew he did not pay attention to that kind of stuff at the office. He introduced me to his wife, again, even though we had met several times. Mrs. Mack and I exchanged pleasantries and gushed our compliments. I guess this is the night for small talk all evening.

As I wandered off to see if I could find any of my coworkers, I looked around the tastefully decorated room. Little twinkle lights were every-where, but not overdone. The banquet tables were nicely decorated with candelabras and greenery but devoid of the foods. They had hor d'oeuves already set out with crackers, cheese, stuffed mushrooms, and various vegetables with dip. I was personally waiting for the main meal.

I felt a presence next to me. "Hi Susie. Do you remember me? I'm Daryl." Oh gosh, it was that yummy guy that I have kept an eye on for the past couple of years. He was the son of one of our lead attorneys.

"Hi Daryl. Of course, I remember you," as I extended my hand. "I thought you were out of the country and not expected back."

"I came in to surprise my Dad. There is not much you can get over on the old man," he said with a chuckle. "I think he was kind of expecting me. May I get you a drink?"

"Yes please, red wine. Wait, actually make that white wine." As Daryl walked off, I realized that I did not want to have a glass of red wine near me with this gorgeous dress on. This was not the night I want to be clumsy. I had no idea that Daryl knew who I was. His sudden appearance at my elbow was unnerving. It is interesting that you can imagine this dreamy guy meeting you some day but when it becomes a reality, you can become a blubbering idiot. Please don't let me blubber!

Daryl brought the drinks over to a bar table that I had selected to stand next to. As we began our small talk, I could feel the eyes of the office girls on me. I was trying so hard to look nonchalant. I asked Daryl about his school, his travels and anything that I could think of so that the conversation would not stall. He was such a gorgeous man to feast your eyes on, that I had not expected him to be so interesting. I found myself leaning into our conversation about his travels and why he was going for the degree of "International Studies." And I even asked that question.

"Why are you studying international studies? You decided not to go into the family business?"

Daryl threw his head back and laughed. No family business for him.

"My plan for international studies is to go into finance and peace negotiations. I feel that there is a need for globalism and to better understand the current conflicts and how they developed or can escalate. I am idealistic enough to believe that there could be unity and peace in the world. I am not sure if this will lead into politics, but I know that even one person can change things in the world."

"Wow, I am so impressed. And yes, I agree that even one person can change the environment and the world. We have seen that constantly, and if anyone could do it, I believe it is you. I love your enthusiasm and your confidence. I cannot wait to follow your career. And obviously you love to travel too," I said with enthusiasm. Gosh, this guy is amazing.

We were having such a great conversation that we did not realize that we had attracted some of the office girls hanging around to listen. I felt obligated to introduce them to Daryl. One of the office girls named Natalie, sauntered up to Daryl and looped her arm into his, and asked him if he wouldn't mind getting her a drink. Daryl nodded his head in agreement, obviously flustered. Daryl returned to the group with the drink in his hand.

"It is so nice to see you again Daryl" said Natalie. "You must tell me what you have been up to," as Natalie practically dragged Daryl away. As they walked away, Daryl looked over his shoulder at me and shrugged his shoulders.

One of my friends, named Sally, said that they couldn't believe what just happened. The group of coworkers started pelting me with questions. Weren't you talking to that hunk first? Did you come with him to the party? How did you meet him? I felt my face turning red with embarrassment at the insulting interaction that just happened with Natalie. Flustered, I excused myself and went to the ladies' room to freshen up. As I stood in front of the mirror to reapply my lipstick, I felt the anger creep up. Well, if Daryl could be led astray that quickly, then no thank you. It looked like he had a previous relationship with Natalie. Maybe he is just as shallow as most men. But I was enjoying our conversation so much. I was clearly disappointed.

By the time I emerged from the restroom, they were bringing out the entrée foods and the smell was exotic. I found Sally and asked if she had saved me a seat. Of course she did, because she was a great friend. Sally tried to turn the conversation over what just happened, but I wouldn't have it. I told her that I would talk to her later about it, and I did not want that to ruin the night. This is supposed to be a night of celebration and fun. And besides, I just met Daryl. It is not like I was dating him. And we laughed at our own joke.

And we did just that. Sally and I had a great time of laughter, eating fantastic food and much more wine. She complimented me on my fantastic dress.

"Susie, you really do look fantastic. You seem to have changed overnight and you look more at peace with yourself and confident. Did you take a happy pill or what?" Sally joked.

"Actually, I do feel happier than I have been. I have stuff going on, like everyone else, but there seems to be fresh air that has blown in. I can't quite figure it out, but I will let you know when I do. Don't laugh, but I think it's about God," I said. Once I had blurted it out, I knew I couldn't take it back.

"God? You are kidding. I didn't know you were a religious person, Susie."

"I'm not. I mean, I don't consider myself as religious. I go to church on Sunday and I believe in God, but I think I am changing. I think I am ready for more. But I don't know what that means. It's just something I am thinking about."

"Huh." It was a short reply from Sally and a questioning look. I just shrugged my shoulders and turned my head to the dance floor. I could see Daryl dancing with Natalie and Mr. and Mrs. Mack were on the dance floor too. Several of the office peeps were dancing with their spouses or their dates. I suddenly felt lonely. Chuck, one of the office interns that I was friendly with, asked me to dance and I joyfully accepted. He was from the local university and had a great sense of humor. I knew he had a girlfriend, which we had talked about, but she was from a different university in another state. Long distance relationships are hard to navigate. He was a guy that could make me laugh with his antics and I always enjoyed just hanging around with him. You could say, he was one of my guy friends. He felt like a little brother. And laugh we did! We danced and hung around each other for the rest of the night. In fact, Sally and I would dance with Chuck as a three-some on the dance floor for the rest of the evening.

I was feeling pretty tipsy as the night wore on. And so was Sally. I usually do not drink, and it does not take much to make me tipsy. Mr. Mack approached us, just as he was leaving.

"Ladies, are you staying at the hotel tonight? Or are you taking an Uber home?" We gave him one of those dumb looks, as though we had not thought that far ahead. "Let me find out if they have a room available for you. I will be right back." Within minutes, Mr. Mack returned with a hotel key. We were flabbergasted! We tried to protest but we were obviously slurring our words. Oh dear, I thought. I had not been this drunk in years! We gave our profuse thank you and "we will pay you back" promise, as Mr. and Mrs. Mack walked away. I was profoundly touched by his gesture. He is not one to be 'fatherly,' but this smacked with such kindness. Sally and I giggled our pleasure at spending the night here. And we continued our party atmosphere towards the hotel bar after our office banquet had closed. We were having an uproariously great time and I think the bar patrons were enjoying our fun too.

The night came to a close with the 'last call' of the evening, and I was done. I was hoping that I would not have a hangover in the morning. We made sure that Chuck had an Uber to take home, Sally and I went to our room. We slipped under the nice clean sheets and promptly fell asleep. The morning sun streak across the room. Where was I? My mouth felt like I had eaten a bag of cotton balls and my eyes were not willing to open beyond a slit. I need some water. As I sat up and reached over to grab my bathrobe, I suddenly realized that I was not in my own apartment. As I swiveled my thick head around, I realized that I was not alone in the bed. I couldn't quite remember who was with me. Oh, this is bad. Here I am sitting on the edge of the bed with wearing only my under clothes, wondering who was in bed with me. I stretch my foggy brain and said, "Sally?"

"Hum?" said the form with her back to me. Whew!

"Oh, I was just wondering if you were awake," I lied. Boy I felt relieved. "Do you want some water? My mouth feels awful." Sally said that would be great.

I jumped into the shower first and only realized that I would need to put the same clothes back on after I was clean. I did remember that I had my other clothes in the car, but this will do for now. After me, Sally had the longest shower ever! By the time she got out, I was returning to the room after getting my clothes from my car. As I was unlocking my hotel room door, the door from across the hall opened. And guess who was coming out - Daryl. There was an embarrassed moment of silence as we finally said good morning, and in from Daryl's room came a female voice. "Who are you talking to?" I saw Daryl's face turn beet red. I gave Daryl a smirk and went into my room.

Sally got dressed and we both went down to breakfast. We had decided to not go to the hotel restaurant, but instead went to a local breakfast joint. She looked plush in her last night clothes and I looked like I was ready for a day of shopping. What a pair we were. I ordered a German pancake and she had her regular, two eggs over medium, hash browns and white toast with blackberry jam. We talked about how much fun we had last night, and I told her about the hallway meeting with Daryl. Sally and I parted with a hug and we went our separate ways, with each one getting into our cars.

As I was turning left at the light to get onto the freeway, suddenly there was a loud bang, and my car was spinning in a circle. Everything was moving in slow motion as everything was flying around in my car. My shoe hit my head, and then there was blackness.

Chapter Six

AS I WAS TRYING TO OPEN MY EYES, THERE WAS SUCH CHAOS around me. I heard voices speaking over me, but I could not understand the words. I felt such pain in my left shoulder and my head hurt tremendously. I knew someone was trying to get my attention, but I couldn't comprehend the words. I made a croaking noise from my throat. "She is coming around," someone said over me.

Someone with a soft voice, "You are in the hospital. You were in an accident. If you can understand me, squeeze my hand." I felt fingers inside my hand and I squeezed it. "Don't move your head because we have not checked to see if there is any damage to your neck. Can you feel any sensation on your feet?" I croaked a yes. The soft voice replied that it was good news. I was trying so hard to open my eyes more than a slit but it was so blurry.

"You are going to CT to check your head and neck. Is there any chance you may be pregnant?" The soft voice indicated to squeeze her hand

91

once for a yes and twice for a no. I squeezed a hard two times. And I suddenly felt the stretcher move. Down the hallway it rolled. A familiar male voice asked if I was going to be okay. I could not place the voice, who was talking?

I was moved onto the CT table without me moving a muscle. I was instructed not to move as the table slid in and out of the tube and I heard whirling sounds. And back to the stretcher I moved and down the hallway it rolled. I went into my ER room, and I felt so alone. I could feel a trickle of a tear go down the side of my face into my ear. I tried to open my eyes again. I croaked out a name, Angela. There above me, her face appeared.

"You are going to be okay," as Angela's face disappeared. The relief of seeing her face was all I needed. I felt a peace come over me.

It seemed like quite a bit of time went by before a male's voice came into the room saying that they can take the collar off that was around my neck. He introduced himself as Dr. Stitch. I began to give a chuckle at the irony of the doctor's name and occupation.

"Well I am glad that you have not lost your sense of humor," he said. "I get that all the time. As you can tell, you were in a car accident. Evidently, someone ran a red light and T-boned you. Lucky for you, it was on your passenger door instead of your driver's door. You have a concussion from a head injury, from hitting your door and from a flying shoe. I think on the police report it says a flying stiletto." I made a croaking chuckle. Dr. Stitch took a breath and went on to explain that I fractured my collar bone and that I will be very sore for about a month or two. I would need to see an Orthopedic Surgeon to determine if I would need surgery. Surgery? No! This time my croaking sounds were sobs.

"Now don't you worry, miss. Your fracture is borderline whether it needs surgery or whether you are to wear a shoulder splint for approximately 5 weeks. The surgeon is the one to determine that. I will let you rest here for a bit and I will prepare your discharge papers. We are going to sit you up and see how you are doing. Your boyfriend is out here and wanted to see you if that is okay." I croaked. What boyfriend? I think Dr. Stitch thought the croak was an acceptance for the admittance of the boyfriend. I could feel the stretcher end being lifted up and my head became semi-erect. In strolled Daryl, and I fainted.

When I awoke, Dr Stitch was checking my eyes with a light and doing tisk tisk sounds. Dr. Stitch started to explain that I was to spend the night in the hospital so that I could be observed. He was not sure if I was dehydrated or whether the head concussion is more serious. He asked if there was anyone that I wanted to call? Your parents? He chuckled just then.

"I guess I made a mistake about the boyfriend thing. As soon as you passed out, he explained that you work in his father's office and that you know each other slightly. Sorry about that. He was kind of worried about you."

It took a while to be admitted, receive an IV, get pain medicine, get to my hospital room, and be introduced to my nurse for the day. By that time, my parents came blustering in. You could tell that they were discombobulated that their little girl had been in an accident and hurt. I tried to comfort them that I was okay but in fact, my head and my shoulder were really hurting. Actually, my whole body was aching. I felt like I have been in a washing machine. I just wanted to sleep. I begged their forgiveness and asked to be left alone. I was so tired and not feeling well at all. I asked my mom to call Mr. Mack and let him know that I would not be at work on Monday. Then I drifted off to sleep.

When I awoke, the room was dark. It was obviously evening. I remember being disturbed throughout my sleep by the nurse as she took blood pressures and adjusted the IV. I think the only reason I woke up was because I was in intense pain. As I moved to find the buzzer for the nurse, this movement began a shot of electricity through my left arm. Oh wow, that was the wrong arm to move. I groaned as I tried the other arm.

"Susie, let me help you. You want to call the nurse?" I recognized Daryl's voice. What was he doing here?

The nurse came in and knew just what to do. She asked if I needed any pain meds and I nodded my head in a yes. How about something to drink? Again, I nodded yes. She asked Daryl to help out with that as she went to retrieve the meds.

There was a soft light in the room by now. Daryl leaned over with a cup of water with a straw hanging out of it. I parted my dry lips and drank. Wow that tasted good. I finally asked him what he was doing here. He admitted to me that he witnessed the accident. He had not realized that it was me in the car at first, but he became frantic once he reached the car and saw my white face. He admitted that it really scared him.

"I'm going to be fine. You don't need to stay." The nurse appeared at my elbow with the pain meds. I took the meds and began to drift off to sleep. I woke up throughout the night a couple of times. Daryl was no longer there in the room. The nurse wanted me to walk, either to the bathroom or down the hallway. She said that if I could not take care of myself, then they would not discharge me and I wanted to get out of there.

My parents were there in morning to take me home. They wanted to take me to their house, but I insisted that they take me to my own. I did not want anyone fussing around me. It made me nervous to ride in the car again. I asked about my little car, but they said that it was totaled. That made my heart ache. I settled down into my little apartment. My parents graciously went grocery shopping and mom had made spaghetti for the evening meal. With assurances that I would be okay, they finally left. After all, they were only a phone call away, as they repeatedly said often. I knew they meant well, but I don't like people hovering over me. I turned on the television and promptly fell asleep in the EZ chair.

I woke up with a start. The television was still running. I eased myself out of the chair with gritted teeth. Doing stuff with one hand was awful. Going to the bathroom was exhausting. I needed to wear stretch shorts for the next week or so. I went to the kitchen to heat something up, but I really was not hungry. I needed something easy and decided on crackers and cheese slices. By the time I sat down in the chair, I had broken out in a sweat. Oh no, I forgot my water in the kitchen. Maybe I do need someone to help me.

This became my routine for the next couple of days. Each day became a little easier. I kept up with my pain medicine and was able to function a little easier with the pills on board. My Orthopedic Surgeon's appointment was on Tuesday and he said that I had the option of a surgery. The fracture was borderline. I may have a lump on my collar bone if I had no surgery but then again you would have a scar. I opted against surgery and he put a splint on my shoulders. The splint made my shoulders push back and had me stand more erect. It was painful. I would need to wear this for weeks. But I was able to move my left arm better with the splint, at least from the elbow to my fingers.

I worked a half day when I returned to work. I was able to function okay, but I was exhausted after a half day of work. Between my family and my co-workers, I was able to get rides to and from work so that I did not have to take the bus. I believe that I needed to rest so that I could continue the healing process. It was humbling to realize how much I could not do. But every day was an improvement, and by the end of the week, my parents stopped calling and asking if I needed anything. And the best improvement was that I could pull up my pants with one hand after going to the restroom. It used to take forever! I am sure the girls in the office wondered what took so long to go to the bathroom.

My routine was to ride the bus home, stop at the corner market for groceries that I could carry with one hand, fix dinner and get ready for bed. I would fall asleep in the big chair or go right to my bed. I would be asleep by 7:30 or 8:00. I felt like a little old lady with my sleep schedule. And would still need an alarm to wake me up. After the first week, I was able to stop the pain meds and just take over the counter meds for my night time rest.

One night I was violently shaken awake in the middle of the night. I thought it was an earthquake. I sat up and was completely disoriented. I turned on my night table lamp to try to figure out what woke me up. Angela was standing at the end of my bed. I must have jumped ten feet. Angela had an intense look on her face. I looked at the clock on the dresser and it said 12:37.

"Hurry! Come now!" Angela prompted as she started walking out of my bedroom. The only thing I could do was to obey with that kind of intense instruction. I was trying to put my good arm in the sleeve of my bathrobe and slipping my feet into my slippers. By that time, she was standing by my front door.

"Go down the hallway." As I opened the door and started walking, I heard a thump, thump from an apartment at the end of the hallway. As I began to get closer, I heard whimpers and a little voice calling for her mamma. By this time Angela was standing next to the door in question. I looked into Angela face with a questioning look and then automatically knew what I was to do. I began to timidly knock on the apartment door.

"Hello? Anyone inside? Does someone need some help?" I heard a crash and bang as something fell to the floor and broke. I began to knock loudly by this time. I heard a little voice on the other side of the door.

"He is gone now. Let me open the door." I could hear a chair scraping against the hardwood floors as if it was being pushed towards the apartment door. There was a slight thud as it hit the door, a rustle of movement, and then the upper bolt clicked into the unlock position. I could hear the chair scraping again as it was being moved out of the way, and the doorknob began to turn. The door opened slowly, and a little dark-haired girl peeked her big brown eyes through the slit in the door.

"Hi, hon. My name is Susie and I live down the hallway. Is everything okay? May I come in and help?" The door swung open with the silent invitation. This silent little girl pointed to her mother that was crumpled on the hardwood floor in a fetal position. As I went over to her mother, I could evaluate quite quickly that she had been beaten and had facial injuries and she was still unconscious. Obviously, she must have a head injury. I asked the little girl if there was a phone around. She ran into the bedroom and returned with her mother's cell phone and silently handed it over. I dialed 911 and explained the situation and gave the address. I was asked to stay on the phone until help arrived. By this time, I was able to look around the room and saw the destruction of the fight that had ensued. There was cold air rushing in from the open window. The 911 operator was asking if the woman had a pulse, and that was affirmative. The little girl was close by but did not hover. As I looked into this little face, I noticed that she was concerned for her mother but without tearful emotion. This little one was approximately 7 years old and she was holding her mother's hand and waiting. I had the fleeting thought that I would be a basket case, wailing and crying. How odd that she is simply waiting with concerned.

"What is your name? Mine is Susie," I asked trying to sound calm.

"Melanie," she replied.

"Hi Melanie. I looks like there was a fight here. Do you know the person that was here?" Melanie nodded her head in a yes.

"Do you know where there is a blanket for your mom? Could you drag it over for her?" Since the mother had a pulse, I felt it was okay to move over to the open window to close it. As we sat and waited for help to arrive, I tried to say calming things. Soon there was a knock on the door and a policeman arrived with the EMT's directly behind him. I could sense Melanie stiffen with the policeman but did not seem too concerned with the EMT's. They began working on the mom right away, taking her blood pressure and pulse. The policeman gently knelt close to Melanie and asked if her mom's purse was here. Melanie jumped up and ran into the bedroom and brought back her mother's wallet so that the officer could get the mother identification.

"Good job Melanie. This policeman will be asking you some questions and he is safe, so you can tell him anything." I introduced myself to the police and told him that I lived down the hall. He asked how I ended up here and whether I heard anything. I explained how I got to her door (minus the mention of Angela) and how I heard sounds coming from the apartment.

"Melanie, do you have someone that can come to pick you up? Like an aunt?" asked the policeman. Oh gosh, I had not thought to ask that. She nodded her head yes and took her mother's phone and showed him the phone number to one of the contacts. He took the phone and wandered into the kitchen to make the phone call.

The police officer returned and told Melanie that her aunt will be coming shortly. By this time, another officer had arrived and was assessing the scene. The policeman took that other officer into the kitchen to talk to him, away from the child and mother. Meanwhile the EMT's were loading the mother onto a gurney to take her to the hospital. Melanie suddenly had a few tears come down her cheeks as she realized that her mother was about to leave her. By then, her mom was making a few groaning noises. I knelt next to Melanie and explained that her mother was going to the hospital so that they could help her. As soon as your aunt arrives, then you both can decide what to do then. Melanie looked deep into my eyes, as though she was confirming whether I was telling her the truth. Then nodded her head and seemed to be calm. What an amazing kid, I thought.

The aunt arrived within 10 minutes of Melanie's mother leaving and I felt that I could take my leave. The police officer had taken down all my information, in case there were any more questions. I gave the aunt my phone number and apartment number in case Melanie or herself needed me and excused myself for the exit. Once I was in the hallway, I realized there was a crowd of onlookers from the other apartments. I smiled and walked towards my door. Once inside my own home, I leaned against the closed door and took a deep breath. Now that the shock and commotion was over, I could feel my collar bone really begin to throb. It was still dark outside, and I looked at the kitchen clock that announced it was 3:33 am. I wanted to take some pain medicine and go back to bed. I had weaned myself from all the medications, but I must have made a lot of movements while in the other apartment. I must have wrenched it because the pain was intense. I grabbed some crackers and water so that the pills would not upset my empty stomach and went straight to bed. Thank goodness, it was the weekend and I could sleep in. I have a lot of questions for Angela the next time I see her.

Chapter Seven

I WOKE WITH A STRETCH AND A HUNGER FOR FOOD. I HAD slept like a rock and realize that it was 10 am. I never sleep that late in the morning! But after all, I was up for most of the night. As I lay on my back in bed, assessing the activities of the night, I lifted my head off the pillow and saw Angela sitting at the foot of my bed.

"Hi," said Angela. "Good work this morning. I was thinking that we make a good pair, and I would like to send you off on more rescues in the future."

"And a howdy doody to you too. That was scary this morning. Is the mother going to be okay?"

"Yes, she is going to be fine, thanks to you. You came at just the right time."

"You mean you woke me up at just the right time. How did you know that was going on?" I asked.

"Her angel told me."

"You mean you talk to other angels?"

"Of course!" Angela said incredulously. I was realizing that I knew nothing about angels and how all this worked.

"Don't worry, you will learn," said Angela as though she was listening to my thoughts.

"You can read my mind?" I asked in disbelief.

"No, but I read your mannerisms and reactions. You are an easy read," she giggled. I did an eye roll. "I saw that," said Angela.

"Listen, I don't know about any rescue stuff. I can barely move as it is. And I don't want to be put into any dangerous situations," I said.

Angela pretended to be shocked. "Dangerous situations? Ha! I am your protector."

"Well, I don't know how this angel stuff works."

"No worries. Our Father protects us both. He is the One that sends us for any missions. He wants to know if you are willing?"

"You mean I have a choice? It didn't feel that way last night," I grumbled.

"Yes, you have a choice. You always have a choice. But do you trust Him?" Angela asked with intensity.

"Angela, to be honest, I don't know God as well as you. It does not seem like I have a direct link to Him like you do. In fact, I didn't know about angels until you came into my life." I was embarrassed to look Angela in the eyes.

Angela was right next to me by then. Shoulder to shoulder. "Susie, you can trust the Lord." It was a statement with the ultimate truth. I felt it deep inside my belly.

"Yes, I believe you, and yes I believe the Lord. And yes I am willing, as long as you are there with me," I said. Suddenly I felt this feather lightness come over me. And with the lightness, there was heat, all over my body. I felt this gust of wind blow through my bedroom, but there were no open windows.

"What the heck was that?" I asked.

Angela started giggling. "That my dear friend, was the Spirit, confirming your commitment." And Angela was gone....again. That was going to take getting used to. The coming and going.

For the rest of the day, I contemplated what that conversation was all about. I decided to get my dust-covered Bible out and look up some things. I was not going to look up the things you would expect, like angels, etc. I wanted to look up trust and truth. There were tons of references in the New Testament. Jesus talked quite a bit about it. Before I knew it, it was dinner time and I realized that I had not eaten since the crackers earlier this morning. I would say that I was ravenous.

I tried to call the hospital about the mother's condition, but they would not release any information. I will wait until tomorrow and walk down to their apartment. I'm sure there are some adjustments that are being made.

Tomorrow was Sunday and I was excited to go to church. This was a first! I always felt that it was more of a duty but there was an excitement that was rumbling in me. I was also looking forward to our Sunday dinner with the fam. I kind of wanted to chew on my brother's ear about God stuff. I probably should go to his church if I were going to ask him any questions. Kind of like making an investment. How am I going to 'withdraw' information if I do not make a 'deposit?' I gave myself a chuckle over my inside joke.

I woke up bright eyed and bushy tailed the next morning. I had already laid out the dress that I was going to wear, something easy to get into but that still looked nice. I wore my brace on the outside of my dress, like a warning signal to anyone that tried to shake my hand or give me a bear hug. I would get tired of telling people that I was in an accident, but it was much better than the pain they inflicted when they gave me a shoulder tap at the joke they made, or a hug. I took my Bible with me this time, excited that I would rustle those pages like the churchy people do.

My brother, Jeffrey, was preaching that day. The worship was outstanding today since they had hired a new music minister. He was really jazzing things up. The scripture reference for the sermon was John 14: 1, "Do not let your hearts be troubled. Trust in God; trust also in Me." I couldn't believe that this was the subject that I most wanted to hear about and learning. Jeff outlined why we should trust in the Lord, that He is trustworthy, and He will never let us down. He expanded on everything I read yesterday. It was like puzzle pieces that were coming together into a nice pattern. It was beginning to make sense. This was why I gave my yes to the Lord. I was beginning to trust Him. I almost wanted to stand up and cheer as Jeffrey ended his sermon with a prayer.

Everyone was filing out of the front doors when I felt a tap on my shoulder (the good shoulder). As I turned to see who was catching my attention, my mouth dropped open seeing Daryl standing there.

"Hi Susie," he shyly said. "How are you feeling? Is your shoulder healing?"

"Hey Daryl, I'm surprised to see you here. Yes, my shoulder is healing simply fine. I felt foggy for a few days because of the concussion but I am good now. Do you go to this church?"

"It's a fluke that I am here today. I was looking for a local church before I head back to school and this was close by. You must live close by too?" Daryl inquired.

"No, I live across town, but this is my brother's church. He is the pastor. I come here occasionally to cheer him on." Daryl laughed at my joke and seemed to relax more.

"Do you have anywhere to go after this? Do you want to get a bite to eat? Daryl inquired eagerly. Just then my brother approached us. I introduced them and briefly told Jeffery how we knew each other.

Jeffery asked if I knew when dinner was supposed to be? I actually did not know, and I was going to call mom later. "Would you mind doing that for me, so I know what time to show up?"

"Sure" Jeffery replied. "I'll be right back."

Daryl and I made small talk as we waited for Jeffery to return. I asked Daryl when he was leaving for college and he replied that he was leaving in a couple of days. I did not have the attraction for this hunk of a guy any longer. I was not sure if it was the accident and him seeing me at my worst, or the fact that I saw him leave the hotel room. I think Daryl was used to women "fawning" over him, but I was clearly not doing that. Is that the only reason he asked me out to lunch? Why didn't I just say no?

Jeffery was returning with his cell phone in hand. "Mom has lunch all ready for us. Daryl, why don't you join us, if you don't mind being cross examined by the family," he said with a mischievous grin. Jeffery knew automatically that this was making me uncomfortable. This was the big brother's ultimate tease. I am going to have to think of a good payback for this one.

Of course, Daryl accepted. Why wouldn't he? My parents were ecstatic that I was bringing a guy with me. I was determined not to let this fluster me. Daryl rode in my borrowed car with me to my parent's house. I had borrowed my Grandmom's car for the weekend and that worked out well for me. As we arrived, the usual pleasantries were offered with a glass of wine, or coffee. Daryl chose the coffee, as did I. As the food was put onto the lazy-susan in the middle of the table, we all took our seats.

"What is this in the middle of the table?" asked Daryl

"You mean the lazy-susan? Dad made it so we didn't have to pass the dishes around. You place the food dishes on it, and it rotates around for everyone to dish themselves up."

"This is brilliant." Daryl was enthralled with this gadget. We were pretty much dished up by the time he finally started to dish up. He just wanted to watch the thing go around. We are so used to the thing, we forgot how wonderful it is, until we have someone over who has never seen it. Everyone was pelting Daryl with questions, about school, family etc. Thank goodness they were asking the questions and I was learning a lot.

Jeffery inquired, "So Daryl, you were the one that saw the accident with Susie and was at the hospital with her?" Off we were into another subject.

After a pause in the conversation, I asked Jeffery, "Hey, Jeff, do you know anything about angels?" There was suddenly silence in the room. No more forks scraping on the plates, no more whirl of the lazy-susan, and all conversation stopped. My dad had his fork halfway to his mouth and stopped in midair.

Jeffery looked at me as though I had horns growing out of my head. "What brings this up?" he asked. Daryl was looking around the table to see if this was normal conversation. It was not.

"Oh, I don't know. I ran into a friend of mine that talked about seeing angels." I tried to sound nonchalant but was not sure if I was pulling it off.

"Don't tell me that you are seeing angels," remarks Jeff. "Maybe it was your concussion." Everyone seemed to enjoy his joke. "Actually, there are quite a few references in the Bible about angels. They are considered messengers and protectors. It is an interesting subject but not one I have dealt with and have investigated. So, your friend says that they see angels? That is fascinating. I have heard of some people seeing angels or demons but have never met anyone that has."

"Demons?" my mother balks. "People see demons? I would never want to see that!"

"I have seen a demon before," Grandmom says. Once again there was a cold silence in the room as everyone stared at Grandmom. "Well, I have! Don't look so shocked." Everyone started asking questions at once. Where did you see it? What did it look like? Was it scary? Did it try to scare you? What happened?

Grandmom held up her hands in surrender. "Now wait a minute! It happened after your father was born. I was sitting in his room during a middle of the night feeding and it was standing by his crib. I got so angry that I told it to go in the name of Jesus. I never saw it again after that."

"What did it look like Grandmom?" I inquired.

"It was a short ugly thing. It was really creepy." Everyone around the table seemed to be chewing on this new information, more than they were chewing on their food. I could feel the unbelief and the concern over Grandmom. Mom and dad kept giving each other glances as though they were unsure about this new information. I was feeling thankful that Mary was not at this luncheon. She would have grabbed onto this new-found information and wanted to investigate further, in a New Age way. I was not sure what I was feeling. I see Angela but I have never thought about the other side of the spiritual world, the demonic.

"Jeff? What do you think?" I asked. I wanted an opinion from an expert.

"Grandmom, how do you know it was a demon? You could have just nodded off and was dreaming." Grandmom's look could have bore holes into Jeffery's head.

"I know what I saw," snapped Grandmom. And that closed the book on this conversation according to Grandmom. You could tell that she was miffed that someone was doubting her.

"Grandmom, I believe you," I said reassuringly. If she only knew what I have experienced. It was obvious to me that Jeffery did not have a belief in seeing into the spiritual realm. He is a good theologian but not so good about understanding or knowing about the supernatural. I understood now that I could not trust Jeffery with my new experiences. I was still trying to wrap my head around this whole angelic thing. And why can I see Angela now? Is there something that changed in me? I am not upset about seeing Angela, but I am trying to logically explain why I can see her, in this stage of my life. I was going along in life quite merrily before all this happened. Angela said that I had a choice. And on the other side of the coin, so did God. He chose me. Now that is a weird thought. He chose me! I suddenly felt warmth overflow me. It was really quick and then it was gone. It was like a confirmation of what I was thinking. Was that the Holy Spirit again? I wanted to talk to Grandmom about this, but I will need to call her at a later date. I looked over at Daryl and he had his head down and was concentrating on his eating. I could just imagine what he thought about all of this. Well, this certainly was a conversation stopper.

The conversation turned to sports and particularly football. Everyone felt relieved to switch to a different conversation. Daryl participated in this subject enthusiastically since his college, Clemson University, is one of the NCAA top scorers. It is doing very well in its football standing and looking good for a championship. Clemson is a hard college to get into and your academic grades must be top notch. Once again, Daryl was impressive. But Daryl lives clear across the country and I do not have time for this; no long-distance relationships!

After the dishes were cleared away and washed, I made excuses to the folks and ushered Daryl out to the car. I was getting tired and wanted to get home to rest and get ready for the week. I dropped Daryl off at the church where his car had been left, said a pleasant good-bye, and headed home. I felt drained from the activity of the weekend. As I went down the hallway of the apartments, I took a detour to the apartment door down the hall. I was wondering how the little girl, Melanie was doing and hoping that her mother was okay. I knocked on the door and there was no answer. I was not surprised.

I made myself a cup of lavender tea and watched out the window as dusk was approaching. It gets dark earlier and earlier. The winter bite of cold was coming in and frosting up the windows. As I sat at my little kitchen table by the windows that overlook the street below, I felt warm and content. It was truly a full weekend. I was replaying the conversation around our dining table about the demonic, the angelic, and seeing into the spiritual realm. Is it normal to do that? Am I the only odd ball? How do I manage this new sensation? Sensation is not the right word, more like ability. A better question would be, is it manageable?

As I sat at my little table, I saw movement out of the corner of my eye. I swiftly turned my heard just in time to see a little squat creature across the room by my bedroom door. I froze in disbelief. We both stared at each other. But he was grinning. I suddenly remembered what Grand-mom said.

"Go in the name of Jesus. You are not allowed in my house." I saw this creature begin to shrink and go towards the outside wall, and then it was gone. What the heck had just happened! I could not believe that the words I said could make such a difference and poof it was gone.

"Angela!" I had a high-pitched squeal coming out of my mouth. And she was suddenly sitting next to me. I started telling her about what just happened, and she sat there nodding her head.

"I know," Angela said. "He shows up here once in a while to interrupt and hijack your dreams. I am glad that you finally have seen him. And I am proud of you for remembering what your Grandmom said. Susie, listen very carefully to this. Jesus' name is very powerful. Everyone has to bend their knee to His Name. Do you understand this? But it is not a name to be used lightly or carelessly. It is a name that you must understand is powerful and you must believe in this Name to be able to use it. Do you understand?" I shook my head up and down. "And another thing, Susie, I do not always come just because you call me. I am obedient to the Father first. I have assignments. You just cannot call me to answer a question or just to talk. But you must know that I hear you all the time and that I am around. Right now, I am here to teach you about the Name. Study Him, and His love and grace. That is the most important thing. Even more important than seeing." There was a long pause as this began to sink in. "God bless your night." Then I was looking at air. Angela was gone. Jesus, the name that is so powerful. His name made that demon leave. And Angela, my angel, has assignments? She obeys God first. The more I know, the more I realize how much I don't know. What a conundrum.

I felt this sudden urge to pray and talk to God. I bowed my head and began to thank God for keeping me safe during the accident. I thanked Him for letting me see Angela and thanked Him for sending the demon away. I prayed for my Grandmom, my parents, Jeffery and Mary. I prayed for the lady down the hallway and her little girl, Melanie. I also prayed for the heart of the girl we found in the alleyway that was being assaulted. In conclusion, I prayed for a good night's sleep and a desire to know Him better.

The was the longest prayer I had said in a long while. I felt refreshed but peaceful. I grabbed my Bible and wanted to read a chapter or two of the New Testament. I felt this desire to know more about Jesus and what He did on earth. I knew some of the stories from Sunday school but those were just stories. I wanted to know what He truly did, and to do that, I needed to read what His disciples had experienced. I wanted to read the very words of that man, Jesus.

Chapter Eight

CHRISTMAS WAS RIGHT AROUND THE CORNER, AND excitement was mounting. The week moved along at great pace at work, and I seemed to really enjoy just having a new release on life. I had realized that I was extremely fortunate to have survived my car crash with basically minor injuries. I had to go to the junk yard to collect my personal items from my totaled car. After seeing my car, it was unbelievable that I survived the crash without major injuries. It was so sad to see this car all squished up. I actually shed a tear seeing it.

Daryl stopped by the office later in the week and asked if I could stay after work tomorrow and go to the downtown Christmas tree. He said that he had another surprise for me too. It sounded like fun and it was nice to be asked out on a date. It was flattering. But I knew that this would be more of a friendship thing, which is great for me.

The next day, I wore my warm coat to work and brought my fleece lined winter boots. If we were going to be out in the evening air, it would be chilly. Daryl arrived a half hour before work was over, so that he could stop in and say hi to his dad. Natalie was also there when he walked into the office. She gushed a hello. Daryl was polite but firm to unravel himself from her attentions. It was an interesting scene to observe, and I tried to conceal a smile as Daryl tried to get out of his uncomfortable situation.

As everyone was leaving the office, Daryl was sitting in the breakroom, waiting for me to finish up on a project. As I walked into the breakroom, with my coat over my arm, Natalie was sitting at the table with Daryl, pouting. Daryl looked relieved that I can come into the room and helped me get my coat on. As I turned to leave, I said a good night to Natalie and watched her mouth hang open. Gotcha! I couldn't help this small amount of glee come bubbling up as I watched her disappointment.

As Daryl and I walked to the Pioneer Courthouse Square, he looped his arm inside of mine. The square is a large brick courtyard that takes up the entire block of downtown. The huge and decorated Evergreen tree is stationed in the center of the courtyard. It is breathtaking and lovely. This year, the tree is 75 feet tall and there are always individual groups that take turns singing Christmas carols. There are coffee and hot chocolate kiosks nearby, and the atmosphere is one of celebration and cheerfulness. Daryl asked whether I wanted coffee or hot chocolate and the answer was, of course, hot chocolate please. He took off to get our drinks and asked for me to meet him in front of the Carolers. I couldn't help but keep smiling since we left the office. This was fantastic. As we sipped our chocolate and enjoyed each other's company, Daryl leaned over and whispered in my ear that he has a surprise for me. I arched an eyebrow with a smile. Huh? This sounds interesting.

He motions to me that we need to walk over to the corner. As we are standing on the sidewalk, I was wondering what was going on. Just then, the Max train pulls up to a stop and Daryl signals with a nudge for us to get on. I couldn't help but start giggling with excitement. I am trying to pelt him with questions and guesses of where we are going. Daryl will not say a word, but he was thoroughly enjoying himself. The tram was westbound, and there are numerous places to stop and have fun. The tram stopped just downhill from the zoo and my delight is profound when I realize that we are going to the Zoo Lights. I had not been there for years, and it is a magical place. They decorate the Zoo with lights, figurines, and decorations. It is amazing to walk around and see and experience this wonderful place. I felt like a little kid and we both enjoyed ourselves immensely. We couldn't stop laughing, joking, and enjoying each other's company. I was quite impressed that he was so thoughtful in planning this date.

As the date was coming to a close, Daryl walked me to his car to give me a ride home. As the car was heating up, he asked for my address so that he could put it into his GPS. A fleeting thought crossed my mind, 'I hope that he does not expect to come up into my apartment.' Daryl asked me what I was doing for New Year's Eve and I laughingly said that I had not thought that far ahead. He suggested that we get together and do something. I was non-committable. I think that took him back a step since he is used to girls agreeing with him no matter what. I told him that I really did not know what I was doing but I'd be sure to let him know. And I also mentioned that if he gets alternate plans, don't worry about having to break that date with me. It would be okay. I could tell that he didn't know what to think of this. It seemed to really bother him.

As Daryl pulled up to my apartment building, he parked and left the engine running. He turned his body towards me, as best as he could with the steering wheel in his way. You could tell that he was trying to form his thoughts.

"Susie, are you upset about the Natalie thing?" I frowned at the question. Was I upset? I do not "claim" ownership of Daryl. What bothered me about that whole thing?

"Daryl, I don't think so. At the party, I was a little miffed that you could be led away by Natalie. I thought we were having a great time together and that seemed to end quickly. But I also realized that you would not have been led away unless you wanted to be." Daryl seemed to absorb this with a frown.

"I just want to apologize for when I was coming out of that hotel room." Now it was my turn to frown.

"I don't understand why you are apologizing to me about what you did that night. Are you apologizing for a night of indiscretion? Or are you apologizing that I caught you coming out of a woman's hotel room? I assume that it was Natalie's room."

"Yes, it was Natalie's room. I feel horrible about that. It was a really stupid thing to do and I regret it. And you are right, I am not sure why I was easily led away by her. I was really enjoying the night just hanging with you. I am asking for your forgiveness, for any hurt that I may have caused you," said Daryl sincerely.

"Of course, I forgive you. And thank you for being concerned for my feelings. And yes, I thought you were stupid," as we both laughed. "Thank you for a lovely evening. I really enjoyed myself." Daryl walked me to my apartment door, and he was being a complete gentleman. I guess he wanted to prove something to me. But it didn't really matter. He felt more like a friend to me than a date. We said our good night and all that stuff, and I let myself into the apartment. I really did have a nice time, I thought with a smile. And Daryl is a great guy. I figured that he just learned some lessons on this trip home.

Christmas day was on a Thursday this year, which meant a four-day holiday. The office always closes early on Christmas Eve, I think so the bosses could run out and shop real quick for their significant-other. I needed to stop by the grocery store to pick up my groceries for the Christmas dinner at my parent's house. I also had run out of wrapping paper, so I had to add that to my list. This year I made out like a bandit for our dinner because I put down to pick up dessert. I had already pre-ordered two pies from a pie shop. Easy peezy. Tonight, Jeffery's church was having a Christmas Eve service and I was really looking forward to it, which is a new feeling for me. I was able to kick off my shoes for a bit and have a cup of tea before getting ready for the evening. I was still driving Grandmom's car and I needed to get it back to her. I was planning on going car shopping after the holidays, especially now that the insurance payment has come through.

The church was surprisingly crowded for a Christmas Eve service. The church was decorated with a Christmas tree in a corner of the raised platform in front. There was greenery on each one of pews and many more candles by the podium. As you entered the church, a person was shaking hands and giving out programs. Another person on the other side of the doorway, was handing out bookmarks that had a scripture printed on it as a gift. There was a festive air about the place and the kids were full of excitement. The church choir, in their formal choir gowns, were already on the raised platforms at the front of the church. I quickly found a place to sit, even though I had to squeeze into the middle of the row. I tried not to step on any toes as I moved into the middle. As I settled myself in, I felt a tap on my shoulder. I turned to see a grinning Daryl. He chuckled at my surprised look. Next to him was sitting a nice-looking woman and a few people down was his father. I gave a curtesy wave to his dad and smiled at Daryl with a nod and turned away as the choir broke open the ceremony with joyous hymn of praise.

The service was absolutely wonderful. The story was told of the birth of Jesus out of the book of Luke in the Bible and the songs that the choir sang were amazing. I actually got teary eyed at the story of Jesus. This was the first time that I realized what He must have given up in order to come to earth. Then there was an invitation for the children to come up to the front for small gifts to be handed out. Pastor Jeff played Santa. There was excitement from the kids as they unwrapped their little gifts.

As the service ended, I turned to Daryl so that I could be properly introduced to his lady friend. Extending my hand towards her, Daryl introduces Ruth, his cousin to me. His cousin? I kind of inwardly laughed at my mistake.

"Welcome to the church. This is the first time that I have come to a Christmas Eve service," I said. This seemed to surprise them.

She asked, "Don't you usually come because it is your brother's church?" I explained that I was not a regular church goer until recently. I expressed that I am beginning to love it though. As we chatted, Jeffery came up and introduced himself to the cousin, shaking Daryl's hand automatically, but his face was riveted on the cousin. I was watching Jeffery and he was completely besotted by Ruth. Daryl and I just stood by and watched as they could not take their eyes off each other. Daryl and I glanced at each other, grinning. This is an interesting development. We were enthralled at watching the two of them try to awkwardly to keep a conversation going. It was like watching a train wreck as it began to happen. After a few minutes, Daryl must have felt sorry for the mess and came to the rescue. I had never seen Jeffery so tongue-tied or trying to fumble through a conversation. He is usually so elegant.

Daryl asked if anyone wanted to go for dessert at the 24-hour restaurant down the street, and everyone hastily accepted. Jeffery excused himself so that he could change out of his Santa costume and told us that he would meet us there. Daryl asked if I needed a ride, which I declined. I would rather leave for home after the dessert.

The restaurant was a busy place considering that it was Christmas Eve. It took a while to be seated. As we were finally getting a table, Jeffery strolled in looking more like himself, except he decided to keep the Santa cap on his head. He shook a few parishioner's hands as he walked through the restaurant, wishing them a Merry Christmas. We ordered our pies and decaf coffee, and made small talk. Jeffery was mostly interested in Daryl's cousin. Ruth lived in the adjoining city of Estacada. Jeffery was intent on finding out about Ruth, her education, her job, her family, etc., and before we knew it, an hour had flown by. The conversation began to stall, with apologies, for not including Daryl and I in the conversation. You could tell that Daryl didn't seem to mind not having the attention on himself. He began to tease Ruth about all the attention she was getting from Jeffery. This made her blush, and Jeffery blustered his apologies. I loved seeing Jeffery being awkward.

"I need to get going anyway." I exclaimed. Jeffery offered to pay the tab and we gushed our thank you. Daryl said that he would leave the waitress the tip. As we were walking out to the parking lot, Jeffery handed Ruth his business card and asked her to call him to have coffee. I felt a joy in my stomach about him doing that. Finally, Jeff was getting interested in someone.

In the parking lot, we had walked into a heated argument that was happening between two men. Our little group stopped in our tracks at the verbal assault that was going on. We could see other people standing near the sidewalk watching what was happening. No one seemed to move to try to stop it or get involved. Suddenly, one of the men pulled out a gun and shot the other man. The atmosphere erupted in terror.

The women were screaming, and the onlooking men were frozen in their tracks. The man that had the gun suddenly took off running down the large parking lot. No one seemed to be chasing him. I felt my legs moving me towards the man that was laying in a pool of his own blood. I had not even realized that I made the conscience effort to move towards him. It was like my body was reacting before my brain was engaged. I heard someone yell, "Call 9-1-1."

I was kneeling by the body of the man as the police arrived. My hands were pressing on the bleeding wound on his chest and the man's eyes were blankly staring up at me. I remember those eyes and the blank stare of death. It was as though he was expressing the disbelief of being shot. I felt a gentle hand under my elbow, trying to lift my hands away from him, and the policeman was whispering in my ear, that there was nothing we can do for him right now. As I shakingly stood up, I felt the wet tears on my cheeks. Someone handed me a handkerchief for my blood-soaked hands. As I moved away from the body, my body began to tremble at what had just transpired. I could not wrap my head around all this violence. Jeffery had his arm around my shoulders and was trying to walk me towards his car. As I sat in his passenger seat, I finally let go and began to sob. I could hear the police interviewing Jeff, Daryl, and Ruth about what had transpired.

Jeffery drove me home, with Daryl driving my car and Ruth following. I couldn't remember getting home but was suddenly in my living room with Daryl handing me a cup of tea. I had finally stopped shaking and had calmed down. Jeffery was asking me whether I would be okay for the night.

"Of course, I will be okay. I'm fine," I reassured everyone. I was feeling more in control of myself, and just wanted everyone to leave. I wanted to be alone. Jeffery said that he would call me in the morning, and he would be happy to drive me to mom and dad's for Christmas dinner. I inwardly groaned at the thought of being with the fam after what just happened. I just nodded my head up and down. I felt a kiss on my forehead and Jeffery telling me that he was proud of me for trying to help that man.

I locked the door after everyone left and I felt drained and dirty. I took another gulp of tea and went into the bathroom to take a shower. As I felt the warm water slide over my body, I began to cry again. Then the deep groaning of painful weeping racked my body. I stood in the shower until the water ran cold. How could life be cut short so quickly? The questions of "why" had begun, without any answers.

I got ready for bed and knew that I would have difficulty getting to sleep. I rummaged through my nightstand and found a Benadryl. "This should help," I thought, and it did. I didn't remember falling asleep, but I do remember the nightmares that kept me tossing and turning throughout the night. I would feel my body jerk at the replay of the gunshot. I had a dream that I was wearing cement shoes that prevented me from helping, and then another dream with me jumping in front of the bullet and me falling into darkness. I woke up with the weariness of a difficult sleep. I tried to climb out of the fogginess with a cup of coffee, which helped somewhat. I made some toast to ease the rumbling in my stomach. The rumbling was not from hunger, it was from the replay of the tragedy that happened last night. I did not want to vomit at the horror of it all, and the toast seemed to settle my flopping stomach.

Could I have tried to prevent this? The thoughts were random and inconclusive. I felt the tears begin to wet my eyes once again. I could feel my heart sink into depression.

"Angela? Are you here?" I whined. From the living room, an answer came. I took my coffee cup and went in to sit on the sofa. "I don't understand what happened last night. Did you see it?" Angela nodded her head.

"Angela, could you have prevented it?" Angela shook her head no.

"It was not my place to prevent it. And it was not yours either." There was a long moment for me to absorb this. "Susie, the loss of life is always tragic. Father never wants His plans for them to be cut short."

"Plans? I don't understand," I said with curiosity.

"Everyone has a destiny to walk out in their lives. The Father has plans for each one of us."

"Does God have a plan for me, Angela?"

"Oh yes," was her answer. I looked deep into Angela's eyes, waiting for her to answer more. She did not comply. I felt that Angela did not give full answers.

"Well?" I asked, feeling a bit exasperated.

"Go to the Spirit about that. It is not my place to give you the answers. It is your place to dig into the mysteries that He has for you."

"But I don't hear from Him like you do." Angela threw back her head and laughed.

"Well, it's about time that you do." And then she was gone. Geez! Whenever I talk to Angela, she brings up more questions that she does answers. What does she mean, "dig into mysteries"? How am I supposed to do that? Just then I hear a thud in the bedroom. Curiously, I walk into my bedroom and I find my bible on the floor next to my nightstand.

"Ha, ha Angela." She has a good point though. I have heard preachers talk about the Bible and how it has all the answers to any questions that we may have. How can the Bible have the answer to why someone shoots another human being? I knew that I had a lot to learn and if there is this "plan" thing, I need to find out what it is all about.

Chapter Nine

TODAY IS CHRISTMAS DAY. MERRY CHRISTMAS TO ME, HO, ho, ho. I guess this is a Christmas I won't soon forget. As I sat on my bed with my Bible in my hand, I began to contemplate the meaning of life. Like so many philosophers that I have learned about in college, they would have theories about the meaning of life, and why we were on earth. The humanists would explain it one way, the atheists and agnostics would explain it in another. And the religious Bible-thumpers would have a whole different view all together. I wanted to find out for myself what the meaning of life was about. I am not in a classroom, where I have to take someone else's word for it, and be tested on it. I want to find out for myself. But I want to find out what God says about the meaning of life. Oh geez, does this mean I will turn out to be a Bible-thumper? Please no. Can't I just be a believer?

I began to read the Jesus story in the book of Luke. I listened to it being read last night at church, but I want to absorb it for myself. The time flew by as I began to eat up the pages of Luke. I was shocked at how much I was enjoying the story. I had so many questions. I realized as I read Luke, that there was so much I needed to learn. I would stop in mid-paragraph and go off into another rabbit- trail. For instance, Luke talked about Elizabeth getting pregnant with John, even though she was old and had never had children. But then it says that John will go before the Lord, "in the spirit and power of Elijah, and to make ready a people prepared for the Lord." I did not know or understand about Elijah. I knew he was an Old Testament prophet, but did not understand why John had to have Elijah's power. Now I was off onto a hunt about Elijah. Before I knew it, I was reading the Bible for hours, and I had not even gotten past Chapter One of Luke. The chapter talked about the angel Gabriel, and I have had experience with an angel, but I was not frightened like Zechariah or Mary. Are there angels that would scare you? Or are there ones that had more power than Angela? So many questions.

Before I knew it, it was time to leave for my parent's house. I jumped into the shower, got dressed, and gathered up the gifts that I was bringing. As I was walking down the hallway, I suddenly realized that I forgot the pies that I was to bring. I ran back to get them, and down the hallway I went. My arms were loaded down with gift packages and pies, and lo and behold Melanie was coming out her apartment door. She was holding onto her mother's hand as her mother was pulling a suitcase behind her. Melanie ran up and gave me a hug.

"Mom, this is the lady that I told you about, who helped us." Her mother gave me a shy smile. She looked like her face was healing and the bruises were not as purple. We exchanged "Merry Christmas" and Melanie told me that they were moving into her aunt's house. I was not able to chat for long since I was already running late, but I was curious about the attack that night. I was thankful that her and her mother were going to a place where they will be safe.

"Did they ever catch the guy that attacked you?" I asked Melanie's mother. She nodded her yes.

Melanie spoke up and said, "It was my dad." Clearly her mother was embarrassed about this information. I reached out my hand and patted Melanie mom's arm.

"I am so sorry. I am thankful that you are doing okay, and you are going to somewhere safe. And you are protecting your beautiful little girl. Melanie, I am going to miss you. Have a wonderful Christmas," I said, as we waved our goodbyes. It was weird that if I had not forgotten the pies, I would have never found out what had happened to mother and daughter.

Arriving at my parent's house, I could sense the relaxed atmosphere. Eggnog was flowing, scented candles were lit, and the fire in the fireplace was spitting sparks. Everyone had already arrived: Jeffery, Grandmom, Mary and Mary's guest Damien. I was finally going to meet this guy she had been dating. As I entered the house, everyone stopped talking. I greeted everyone with a Merry Christmas. Jeffery must have already told them about last night's events. They began to treat me as though I was fragile, but I assured them that I was feeling okay. Jeffery helped me out of my coat and asked if I was able to sleep last night. I told him that it was a rough night, but that I felt better this morning.

My first impression of Damien was that he was handsome, and he knew it. It was quite obvious that Mary liked Damien, but I wondered if the feelings were truly mutual. There was something that made me cautious around Damien, and I could not quite put my finger on it. Damien was chatting with my dad and they seemed to be getting along well. They were talking about my dad's favorite subject, football. Mary was on the sideline with a pleased look on her face, trying to follow the conversation even though she knew virtually nothing about football. I went into the kitchen to greet mom and put away the pies. My mother was busy putting the dinner's final touches on. The turkey was sitting out on top of the counter, and its wonderful aroma streamed through the warm kitchen. I asked my mom if she needed any help, and she nodded her head and directed me to take the stuffing out of the turkey and put it into a dish. She had already drained the drippings and was busy making gravy. My mouth was already beginning to water with anticipation. I love turkey dinners, even though I just had one a short time ago at Thanksgiving. Once the dressing was in the serving dish, I was directed to put the mashed potatoes into a dish and start setting everything on the wonderfully decorated table. Mother went all out in her decorating and table-setting. She had her mother's china out, and the silverware had been polished. Mom didn't make conversation in the kitchen and must have known instinctively that I just wanted to keep quietly busy. Once all the food was put onto the table and she was about ready to call everyone, Mom pulled me aside and asked if I was doing okay. I could see the concern in her eyes.

"I'm fine Mom. Thanks for asking, but I don't want to talk about it." Mom nodded her head in agreement.

"But honey, if you ever want to talk about it, I'll be right there for you."
I smiled in return and felt my heart grow with love. I knew my mother
meant well, but I also knew that she was incapable of understanding the
depth of my feelings about last night's events. I was still trying to wrap
my head around them. Somewhere there was a family out there that did
not have a dad, brother, or son to be there for Christmas. What a monu-
mental loss that would have been to handle on Christmas day, or any day
for that matter. With that thought, I let out a huge sigh.

Dinner was delicious and the conversation continued to flow, even though
I did not participate. I think everyone understood why I was in a reflective
mood. About halfway through the meal, I couldn't help but watch Damien.
That was easy since everyone was asking him questions and he liked to talk.
But I noticed that a grey smoke would come out of his mouth occasionally.
I was intrigued about this. It was like smoke from a cigarette but lighter and
less dense, if that makes sense. I would pay attention to the words that were
spoken every time a saw the misty haze. A thought would flash through
my mind, is he telling the truth? Mary would lean into him every once in
a while, and I tried to pay attention. Did the mist happen at the same time
that she leaned towards Damien? This was like a mystery that I was trying
to figure out. I tried not to stare at Damien, but I was trying to pay attention.

Suddenly there appeared a creature on his shoulder. I could only see
the creature's vague outline. It sat on Damien's shoulder and wrapped
around his neck towards his back. This creature would whisper into his
ear or around his head. I strained to hear what was being said. Suddenly
the creature looked at me with bulging red eyes and opened his mouth to
strike at me. The creature lunged and I jumped up and knocked my chair

over. Everyone was alarmed at my quick movement... except Damien. He had a slight smile that he tried to hide. And then just as fast, I could not see the creature any longer.

Am I going bonkers? Everyone became worried as I rushed out of the room into the kitchen. I hovered over the kitchen sink and was running water over my hands. I felt cold and sweaty, as though I was coming down with something. My stomach was upset with a quick onset of nausea. What is happening to me? I wanted to leave, but the gifts were unopened, and dinner was still in progress. How do I get out of this situation? Jeffery came in to check on me.

"Are you doing okay Susie? You look whiter than a sheet." I nodded my head while trying to keep my nausea under control. I finally told him that I was not feeling that great.

"I think I just want to go home. I know this is Christmas and everything but I just want to go lay down." Jeffery suggested going to one of the bedrooms in the house and laying down for a bit. But I really felt that I needed to leave this house, since Damien was here. Jeffery wanted to drive me home because I was so white and clammy, but I assured him that I would be fine and if I felt ill that I would just pull over. I would text him when I got home. I rushed through the dining room with a wave of my hand with Jeffery following with explanations. I gathered up my coat and purse and was out the door quicker than a flash.

Once in the car, I took a deep breath and blew it out. I started the car and drove down the block, away from my parent's house. I instantly felt a bit better. I pulled to the curb and shifted the car into park, but left the car running for the heater. I leaned my head forward onto the wheel and just breathed a few breaths of relief. What was that I was seeing on Damien? Or should I be asking if I really saw it or was that my imagination. No! It was not my imagination! The thing lunged at me. That was really scary. After I pulled myself together, I drove the rest of the way home and parked and locked the car.

I went into my apartment and started the water boiling for a cup of tea. I hung up my coat, tossed my shoes in the corner and turned up the heat in the living room. I instantly felt relief, being in my own place. The tea-kettle was beginning to boil, so I headed to the kitchen to insert the tea bag… and guess who was sitting on my counter? Yep, Angela. My relief in seeing her brought tears to my eyes. I tried to hold the tears back but they began to cascade down my cheeks.

"Oh Angela! Did you see what happened? Was I imagining what happened at my parent's house?" I began to shake a bit and the tears and fright began to have its impact on me. Angela suggested that we take the tea to the front room and have a chat.

As I sat on the sofa, Angela's presence seemed to calm me. She waited in silence until I took my first sip of tea and settled down and relaxed in the cushions.

"Are you doing better?" I nodded my head and let out a sigh. "There are a lot of things that were going on at your parent's house. And yes I was there." I began to open my mouth with a question, but Angela lifted her hand up in a "stop" motion. "Let me try to explain a few things to you, Susie. First of all, the Almighty Lord has begun to reveal your gifts. You are beginning to see into the spiritual realm. You see me, but now the Lord wants to show you other things. He has opened this opportunity and it can be scary at first."

"I am not sure I want to see things like that. And Damien, what is he? He must be an evil person."

Angela said, "We do not dislike Damien. He is still one of God's children. We hate what has infected him."

"You mean that creature was infecting him? But Damien kind of smiled when I became upset. I don't understand any of this. Why would he smile?"

Angela replied, "Well, in Damien's case, he actually has partnered with this evil force. I don't think he understands what he has partnered with, or maybe he does. Only God knows the heart and He will let me know if I need to know it. "

I crossed my arms over my chest. "Well, I am not sure I want to see any longer." Angela's face grew sad. "Oh Angela, I didn't mean you!"

"The Lord Almighty has given you a special gift. He loves mankind so much. He wants to have a relationship with each and everyone of us. God loves people, not what is infecting them. Some people do not realize what is infecting them or what they have partnered with. But this gift will help you do warfare."

"Warfare! There is going to be a war!" I said in alarm. Angela began to laugh.

"Susie, I love your sweetness," said Angela. "We have been in warfare since Adam and Eve had to leave the Garden. I know this is a lot to take in, but I need to tell you something really important. None of those creatures can harm you unless you partner with them. You are a mighty warrior. When you are a believer and carry the Name, they cannot harm you. But lesson number two, even believers can believe a lie and therefore accept partnership." My face must have shown the shock. "But that will be a discussion for another time. The best thing you can do, is to pray for Damien and also your sister Mary. They need your help." Angela turned to leave. And then changed her mind. "One more thing, you need to thank God for your gift instead of asking Him to take it away. It is a valuable gift. You will see."

Chapter Ten

I HAD A LOT TO CHEW ON. I JUST WANTED TO GO TO BED, rest and shut out everything that had happened the past few days. I was exhausted and emotionally drained. My emotions were off the charts and I could not seem to control them. I was on the verge of crying but did not have the strength to let it all out. My thoughts were all over the place, shifting from the parking lot murder to Damien. I wondered whether Mary was so involved with him that she couldn't see if he was a good match for her.

As I laid in bed, my thoughts drifted to Damien and Mary. Angela said that Damien was 'infected.' Did that mean that Mary was also infected? Was it like a disease? Did the haze I saw out of Damien's mouth come from a contamination inside him? I knew that Mary was involved in New-Age stuff. Did that attraction to those spiritual beliefs include Damien? Maybe it is time that I asked Mary out for lunch and find out a little more about what she is involved in. I suddenly realized that I have not been such a good big sister. Mary and I have drifted apart, and I am concerned that I may not be able to bridge this Grand Canyon chasm. But it is worth a try. It is never too late to mend a relationship, even if we have grown apart.

Once again, I did not have a good night's sleep. My dreams ranged from gun shots to monsters. There was a dream where I was holding the gun and about to shoot the demon off of Damien, but I missed the demon and shot Damien instead. I woke up in a cold sweat. This is awful. I am finding no peace at night. I looked at the clock and it was 4:20 in the early morning. I decided to get up and make some coffee. I did not want to go back to sleep and dream again.

As I sat at the kitchen table with a steaming cup of coffee, I decided this is a good time to read the Bible. I grabbed a journal just in case I wanted to take some notes. The hours flew by, and I started filling up pages in the journal with thoughts. My thoughts ranged from what the Bible said, to questions I would want to ask God if I was standing in front of Him, and questions I would want to ask Angela.

I was reading the fourth chapter in the book of Luke, about the temptations of Jesus. I know Jesus is God, but I found this chapter fascinating. It produced many more questions. I needed to call Jeffery later. It seemed like the devil did not believe that Jesus was God. And the devil knows Bible verses? Go figure! Jesus knew more about the scriptures at the age of 12 than the teachers in the temple of Jerusalem. Well, after all, He is God.

I called Mary later that day and asked if she could go to lunch. She said Saturday was best for her, which was tomorrow. Perfect! We set a time and place. She was surprised to hear from me and curious why I wanted to have lunch. She was hesitant at first, but then she accepted.

My next phone call was to Jeffery. His voice had a concerned edge to it and he was wondering how I was doing. I told him I was doing okay but not sleeping well at night. He said that his sleep was not that great either.

"Jeff, I have some questions about the Bible. Is there a time when we could meet?" I think my question knocked Jeffery for a loop. He readily said yes as though I would back out. He had a little time today so I invited him over for coffee.

Jeffery arrived a few hours later, with pizza in hand. Just what the doctor ordered! I did not realize how hungry I was until the aroma of the sausage and mushroom pizza entered the house.

We sat at the kitchen table and I made another pot of coffee. At this rate, with all the caffeine, I was never going to get to sleep that night. As we munched on the pizza, Jeffery began to ask me how I was feeling.

"Susie, you have had quite a few eventful things happen to you lately. I would totally understand if you were feeling overwhelmed and could not sleep very well. By the way, how is that lady and her daughter from down the hallway?"

"I saw them the other day." I replied. "They are doing much better and they have moved out to live with their aunt. And yes, there has been a lot going on. But the reason I asked you over is because I have questions about the Bible."

"I have to admit Susie, I was a little surprised at your phone call. I'm not complaining, but are you reading the Bible because of the murder?" Jeffery asked.

"No, but that probably was the tipping point, prompting me to read. There has been a lot that has happened to me lately and someone said that I should find out God's plans for me, and that it is in the Bible." I paused as I tried to collect my thoughts. "But before we get to my destiny thing, I wanted to know why the devil didn't know that Jesus was God."

Jeff's face registered surprise. "Where did you hear that?"

"It is right in Luke, chapter four." I took out my Bible and flipped to the pages that had a bookmark there. "It keeps saying "if" as though he does not believe Jesus is God."

Jeffery began to smile. "That is very perceptive of you Susie. Well, one of the devil's tools is to spread doubt of who God the Father, Jesus, or the Holy Spirit truly is. If you are led to doubt God, then you begin to doubt what the truth is. Let me ask you a question. Susie, do you need to prove to me who you are?" I shook my head no. "Of course not. You know that you are Susie Quade and you know who you are, what you do for a job and also how you develop your ideas and thoughts. If someone points to you and says you are someone else, you know that is not true because you already know who you are. That is the same with God. The devil wants you to believe something else about who God is so that he can lead you down a different path. Make sense? But God knows who He is, and He will not take the bait of having to "prove" who He is, or be tempted to show His power and authority to satan. If you look further on into chapter four, when Jesus begins to take the demons out of people, the demons say that Jesus is the Son of God. They know who He is."

"Jeff, I know that I am a Christian but I am amazed that I don't know much about the Bible. I know some of the stories but I have never really sat down and read it."

"Welcome to my world. This is what I am called to do, to teach and pastor people." Jeff continued speaking passionately. "I would love for people to be able to see God the way I do. He is such a loving and kind God. And He is so patient. He only wants a relationship with us, like a best friend. And He puts that desire in us to search for Him."

We sat there for a few minutes sipping our coffee. "Then why do people go off and do evil things or go to other beliefs?"

"That is a good question. But may I ask you a question? Why did you go through life without wanting to read the Bible?"

Oh dang, that was a good question. I did not want to tell Jeff about Angela, but I began to think about when I did want to read the Bible. "I think it is because I realized that there is more to life than what I was experiencing." Hesitantly I added, "And I believe there is a spiritual world that I don't know about, and I want to understand more."

"Wow, Susie, you are full of surprises. I am glad that you reached out to search in the Bible instead of searching other spiritual books. That road can lead into dangerous ground."

"What kind of spiritual books?" I asked. "You mean like that New Age stuff that Mary is into?"

"Exactly. Like reincarnation and mystical books. I am worried about Mary and what is going on with her. I don't like her being in this New Age spirituality stuff, but I know I need to love her and be available if she needs to talk."

I mentioned that I was having lunch with her the next day. "I want to understand where she is coming from and how she is getting along. It has been a long time since I connected with her. I am ashamed that I have not been a very good big sister. And I am curious about this Damien guy. I was not in a good place yesterday, but he makes me nervous."

We continued to chat about Mom and Dad, and also about being pastor of a church. I asked him about Daryl's cousin, if Jeff was going to take her out for coffee? Jeff expressed that he would love to, but she had not given him a call yet. I asked him if he wanted me to track down her phone number. Jeff thought about that and declined, for now.

As Jeffery was leaving, he gave me a big hug. He assured me that he was there for me, anytime. He would love to take the time to discuss things in the Bible with me, but he also reminded me that after the New Year, the Wednesday evening Bible study would start again. I was welcome to join. I assured him that I would think about it. I did want to learn more, but I was not sure if I wanted to join his study. I wondered if there was something closer to where I lived.

As I closed my front door and locked it, I realized that we never got around to discussing what I wanted to ask him. I wanted to ask how I find out about God's plans for me or my destiny. I know it is not like looking up a recipe, but I know there must be something like that in the Bible.

I slept a little better that night, thanks to a Chamomile tea. I was kind of excited to be meeting with Mary. I knew after seeing Jeff yesterday that I needed to make a conscious effort to connect with her. We had grown apart in so many ways. I did not want this meeting to be driven by guilt but by a desire to become a better sister. Sisters are supposed to care for one another and there seemed to be a disconnect with us. I am hoping that this will begin the repair process.

Mary and I were to meet at a Thai restaurant between her house and mine. I had never been there, but Mary said it had great food. I got there a few minutes early and was seated at a table against the wall. Hot tea and water were set before me and I sat gazing around the room. There were all kinds of Asian decorations and above their cash register was a shelf with a gold statue with fruit on the ledge. Finally, Mary came blustering into the restaurant and plopped herself down in a chair with a huff.

"Sorry I am late. I had a bit of trouble getting out of the apartment. Time just got away from me." Mary said.

"It's okay. I got here a little early and I don't even think you are late. Do you want some tea or water?" I asked. As we looked over the menu, I asked her what was good to eat here. Mary named off a few choice dishes that she liked and we ordered when the waiter came to bring her hot tea.

As Mary cradled her tea in her hands to warm them, she asked me what's up. "Why did you want to have lunch? Is everything okay with you?"

"Everything is good, well, kind of. I have had a few eventful things happen, but I am doing much better. It kind of made me start re-evaluating things in my life, and one of the things I began to think about is my relationship with you. I wanted to apologize to you that I have not been a good sister. I have been in my own world and not paying attention to the important things, like family." Mary sat back in her chair and absorbed this new information. You could tell that it took her by surprise, and she was thinking of what to say to me next.

"I totally get it about being in your own world. I think everyone does that to an extent. And each of us are going through our own growing pains and feeling like we need to do life on our own. Our family is not the greatest about in-depth conversations around the dinner table," Mary reminded.

"Exactly. And I was in my own little world also, even though I didn't mean to be. And that is a good point. If you were to have an in-depth conversation, what would it be about?" I asked. Mary became thoughtful. Just then, our lunch came to the table and interrupted her thoughts. As we expressed our delight in the steaming food before us, the conversation began to divert into trivial matters. As we finished our meal, I guided the conversation back to my original question.

"I think I would talk about what matters in the world. Whether it was political, environmental, or religious. There is so much to discover in the world of knowledge. And there is so much happening in the world, not just our little corner of the nation. Environmentally, we are killing our world with pollution and over-population. We need to educate our fellow man on the environment and being careful to sustain the environment for the next generations. For example, the oceans are becoming polluted. In Asia, the garbage that is floating in the ocean is horrible. It is being discovered how this is affecting the marine life and how we need to curb it." Mary was speaking passionately, and she leaned into the discussion with vigor. I was pleasantly surprised that Mary knew so much about the environment.

"The environment is a huge subject, and you know a lot about it," I agreed. "That kind of discussion could go on many pathways. And there are people on the other side of the issue that would talk about how to keep our economy at this same level of "neediness" and still keep the environment safe. For example, oceanic drilling for oil. Our nation demands oil to sustain what the people desire and sometimes that affects the environment. They make excuses for this and try to keep it safe. And over-population is a whole other subject that can take forever to discuss with many aspects of the problem. Whew! You are right about the depth of discussions we could have." I gave Mary a smile. "Look at us solving the world's problems," as I gave a snort of laughter. It eased the tension that was building with this passionate discussion.

I wanted to redirect the conversation to Damien issue, but I also knew that I needed to be careful. I did not want Mary to become defensive. "How did you meet Damien? Were you nervous to take him to meet the family?"

Mary's eyes lit up with the mention of Damien's name. "We met in a coffee shop. The shop was crowded and there was nowhere to sit. He asked to sit at my table. We started to talk and one thing led to another. He is so smart, and I could listen to him all day long," Mary said dreamily.

"That is great. It is obvious that you like him very much. What do you guys talk about?" I asked.

"We talk about environmental stuff, what is happening in the world, and that everything is fixable through keeping true to your self."

"Keeping true to yourself?" I asked.

Mary let out a giggle. "No not true to yourself, but true to your Self, with a capital 'S'. Your Self can be one with the universe and there is so much to learn from other's experience on their spiritual path. They tap into the spiritual energy of the universe and learn ways to heal the environment, or how to govern, etc. There are so many ways to tap into our own spiritual energy in order to touch God. I have so much more to learn about this and I am just beginning on this journey. I am not an expert, like Damien."

"So, Damien is an expert?" I asked. Mary nodded her head with a smile. "Have you talked to Jeffery about this?"

"No! Why would I? He is on a much different path and would not understand. His mind is closed. I am in the process of opening my mind."

I was beginning to have a sinking feeling about all this. There was something in my inner being that was forcibly resistant to this discussion. I was at a loss on how to turn this around and I felt unqualified to do so. I did not know enough about what Mary believed to contradict her, and I did not know enough about God and the Bible to have a firm foundation. I felt that I was in deep water. I took a deep breath and closed my eyes for a second. What do I say Lord?

"Mary, I don't know about anything that you are learning about. But I do know that I love you. I want a better relationship with you. Let's keep meeting together and really begin a deeper sisterhood," I said earnestly.

"I agree. This has been fun. I really appreciate you reaching out and getting ahold of me. Can Damien meet with us too?" asked Mary.

"Actually, I would rather just meet with you. I want us to have a firm friendship first. That is my priority, first and foremost," I said with a smile and as I said it, I reached out to put my hand on top of her hands. I wanted Mary to realize that I was earnestly seeking this friendship and a new beginning. As our eyes met over the table, we smiled at each other. I could feel her heart begin to open up to me. My heart blossomed with love for Mary in a new way. We are going to make this work!

We agreed to meet weekly or every other week. I asked Mary if she was still going to Mom and Dad's on Sunday for our weekly dinners. She was non-committed to this obligation and was uneasy being tied down. Her demeanor switched visibly, which I found interesting. I wondered if she had a problem with our parents or our family gatherings. I would table that discussion for another time. We gave each other a big hug as we left the restaurant. I felt good about the lunch meeting, as a whole. This was my primary mission, just to let Mary know that I loved her. And I thought I diverted the issue of Damien meeting with us quite well.

I got home from my outing and felt successful. I made a few phone calls to friends, wishing them a Merry Christmas, and asking if they have plans for the New Year's Eve celebration. Everyone was pretty much unsure what they were going to do. A few of them were just staying home and not willing to go out into the madness. Some were willing to jump into the drunken mosh-pit of so called "fun." I was not sure what I was feeling like. I was not really a drinker, and since the company party, I had no desire to be drunk again. I do not like the feeling of being out of control, and once you start down that road, it seems to go skidding into a new slippery slide of its own.

I fixed myself salad for dinner since I stuffed myself at lunch. I turned on the television, and watched a few shows as I surfed the channels. I really did not have a desire to watch TV, and seemed to just be occupying my time until it was time to go to bed. I thought about and replayed my visit with Mary and chewed on some of the things that were said. I was building a bridge with her, but I also knew it was a fragile bridge. Was it a bridge that was strong enough to sustain a disagreement with her and would she agree to disagree and still maintain a relationship? That was ultimately the main question, and only time will tell.

Chapter Eleven

I KNEW THIS WAS GOING TO BE ANOTHER SHORT WEEK OF work. Hallelujah! At the law offices, this meant that we needed to finish any tasks that could not be transferred to the next year, like tax issues and some court-filings. I went into work early on Monday morning to get a start on the heavy workload, since I needed to make up for the days that would be missed at the end of the holiday week. I made a list of things that absolutely needed to be taken care of by Mr. Mack, and made two different stacks of files on my desk. One stack was files for tax issues that needed to be dealt with before the end of the year, and the other stack were the court-filings. The second one was not a large stack since I had been making headway on issues since the end of November. There were only a few meetings on Mr. Mack's schedule, which was normal for after Christmas. Most of our clients were on vacation until the New Year, and as I looked around the office, it seemed like most of the employees were missing too.

Before I knew it, Mr. Mack came out of his office to ask what I was planning to do about lunch. I had forgotten to pack a lunch, and told him that I had no plans. He said that he would pay for our lunch if I would go get it for us. I readily agreed on that fortunate plan. I suggested the food trucks but Mr. Mack turned up his nose at that suggestion. He was thinking of something a little more elaborate. I was all for being spendy! He decided on a Blacken Salmon Caesar's Salad and that sounded so wonderful that I said to make it two. I called in advance to the restaurant and said I would be there in ten minutes.

It was nice to be out in the cool and crisp air, away from the stuffy office. I needed the walk to clear my brain and for once, the sky was clear. There were not many people out on the sidewalk since most of the shoppers were done with the sales and some of the offices were closed for the holidays. I got to the restaurant and paid with Mr. Mack's credit card. As I was walking back to the office, I was thankful that I decided on the salad, since any hot food would have been cold by the time I returned to the office.

Mr. Mack and I ate in the conference room as he regaled me with a funny story of Christmas morning. I had not seen him so animated in a long time, and I was just enjoying seeing him be lively. It was evident that his marriage was on track and his kids were all doing fine. That so pleased me since I really liked Mr. Mack. He could be a bear at times, but it seems that some major stress had been lifted off his shoulders. In a rare moment over lunch, he looked me in the eye and said how much he appreciated working with me. He said I was a "good egg." I mumbled my thanks and gave him a huge smile. It is always nice to be appreciated! It kind of makes you warm and fuzzy inside.

The work week was swiftly coming to a close. Mr. Mack and I had completed all our tasks that needed to be done. Mack had informed me that we did so well, that I could go home early today, which was New Year's Eve. I told him to have a happy New Year and to be safe. He replied that he planned to, that he was going to stay home with the family playing games. Wow, what a switch from the old Mr. Mack. Playing games with the family! Go figure.

I realized that I had not made any plans for the evening and truth be told, it did not bother me. I did not have any desire to go out and party or to drive around in the evening. The possibility of having an accident due to a drunk driver increases substantially and I had been in enough accidents lately. No thank you! I was resigned to stay at home and watch the celebrations on the television. My phone rang and I noticed that it was Daryl's name on the face. As I answered it, mostly out of curiosity, I tried to sound cheerful.

"Hi Susie. Why haven't you answered any of my texts? Are you upset with me?" asked Daryl.

"Daryl, I haven't received any texts from you. Honest! Are you pulling my leg?" My first thought was that he was trying to cover his tracks for the reason of not getting ahold of me, not that I expected it.

"Seriously? I have texted you three different times this week. I was trying to make plans for tonight and I was getting upset that you were avoiding me. I would rather that you were honest with me." I could not help but smile at the reference that my Grandmom would have used; he had a 'bee in his bonnet.'

"I was not avoiding you Daryl. And my phone has been acting up. One of my friends said that they tried to call me, and it would not go through, and it made a weird ringing sound. I am sorry. Don't worry about me though. I didn't make any plans but I am happy to just stay at home. It has been a pretty eventful past few weeks for me," I said with sincerity.

"It's okay." Daryl's voice sounded much calmer. "We were going to get together and just play games tonight. There were a bunch of us that didn't want to go partying but still wanted to meet up. Do you want to join us? I can come to pick you up. Ruth just called your brother, and he is coming over too." Now that was an interesting development! I consented if nothing else but to see what is going to happen between Jeff and Ruth. That would be fun just to watch them! I asked Daryl what the dress code would be, dresses or jeans? He replied that it will be super casual. Perfect! He said that he would be here around 8:00. As I got off the phone, I realized that I better eat something and drink a cup of coffee so that I would not be yawning by 10:00. I had been up early this morning and had gone into the office. I glanced at my watch and realized it was still early and I had plenty of time for a nap.

Daryl was right on time to pick me up. I felt refreshed after relaxing and was excited about the evening. It has been a while since I just hung out with a group, and it will be nice to meet new people. I layered my clothing choices since I did not know where we were going. A nice shirt with a pullover sweater will do the trick. I hate being chilled.

Daryl asked how I was doing, just like everyone else did in my life. There was always "concern" in their voices, but with Daryl it was more like a genuine welfare check. When you have walked through an experience like a murder, and a car wreck together, it seems to have a bonding effect that is like an invisible string attached to each another. Whereas I have been trying to bury some of the trauma feelings that I have had, Daryl was careful to chip away at the layers that I was attempting to erect to shield myself. And he was ever so gentle about it. It unnerved me, his concern, since I had labeled him an arrogant and social preppy guy. In all the other times I had ever seen him, at the company parties, he ignored me. And the feelings of disrespect I had for him confirmed my label as he went with Natalie at the party. But Daryl was showing me a different side of him. I considered him just a friend because I knew I could not fully trust him and did not want him any closer than that. But I realized that there had been a shift in my heart when he apologized for his behavior and asked for my forgiveness. I was not sure why he asked for forgiveness unless he sensed my disappointment in him. Did he want to change my opinion of him? I hope this is not just a show he was putting on. I was beginning to kind of like him and it was scaring me.

We drove up in front of a large house that had many cars parked out in front. It seemed that every light in the house must have been turned on because it was lit up and bright. The front door was enormous and tall. You could comfortably put three ladies abreast in the doorway and we would all fit nicely. It was an ornate carved double-door with etched paned glass in the middle of each door. The front door opened into a large twenty-foot tall foyer with a curved stairway at the far end of the house. To the left of the front door, I could see a library type room with a fireplace blazing, and to the right was a room with a large group of people milling around. The room was huge enough to not feel crowded.

There was a chess board on a table in the far corner of the room with two men playing, oblivious of the crowd around them. On the opposite side of the room were a couple of backgammon games in progress. Decks of cards had been placed on the coffee tables, ready to be played.

Daryl clapped his hands together in the center of the room and brought everyone's attention towards him. "Happy New Year to everyone! Thank you for joining us here tonight. The bar is open, but I want to mention that there is a bowl on the bar for your car keys. If anyone gets a drink, I want you to automatically put your car keys in the bowl. We have a few designated drivers here tonight and they will help us out, but I also want you to be responsible to monitor yourself. We will be playing a few games that everyone can join in, like Fishbowl or Uno but mostly this is a celebration tonight. We are closing out this year and beginning a new season. So, get to know other people that you don't know and have a good time."

As I looked around the room, I could see some girls had dresses on but mostly everyone was dressed casually. I was enchanted with this beautiful house. Obviously, Daryl was in charge of this party and I was wondering if this was one of his relative's houses. Daryl was introducing me to a couple of his friends, some from as far back as grade school, or a previous neighborhood they lived in. He had some long-term friends. It made me disappointed that I did not keep the same friends I had when I was young. I wondered if that would have changed if I had played sports. It seemed like the friends that I had, just grew apart the older we got. We would get boyfriends and then hang out with their friends and drop our girlfriends like hot potatoes. I realized that I need to invest in my girlfriends that I have now, and develop deeper ties.

"Whose house is this?" I inquired. Daryl looked at me kind of funny and told me that this was his parent's house. My eyebrows shot up. Whoa. "And it is no problem to have a party here? Are they here in the house?"

Daryl laughed. "It's not like I am in high school! Yes, they know that I am having friends over, but they are away for the holidays." He paused thoughtfully. "I am respectful of our home. Once upon a time, I was not. That was something I regret deeply. It will never happen again," Daryl said with a grin. "What would you like to drink?"

"I would love a glass of red wine. Thank you." I spotted Jeffery coming in the door and craning his neck over the crowd, searching for some-one. I bet he is not looking for me, ha ha. I had not seen Ruth yet, so I sauntered over to say hello to this newcomer. Nothing like coming into a room full of people and not know anyone. But before I could get to Jeff, several people were calling out to him. Geez, he is much more well known than I thought. As I approached Jeffery, he was surrounded by a group of guys. Some were college age and some a bit older. They were shaking hands and grinning from ear to ear. Jeffery spotted me and introduced me to his basketball buddies. Now it made sense. They began to regale me with basketball mishaps that Jeff was known to do on the court, laughing and punching each other on the shoulder. We were laughing uproariously when Daryl walked up with a couple glasses of wine in his hands. You could tell that he was pleased that everyone was enjoying themselves.

And this was how the night went on, laughing, joking and thoroughly having fun. It was one of the best nights that I have had in a long time.

We ended up playing a game called Fishbowl, that was part charade and part one-word hints. There were several teams involved and we got very loud and competitive. Before we knew it, it was past midnight, and we missed the Ball being dropped.

Daryl took me home at two in the morning and we were still giggling at some of the antics that had happened that night. I know Jeff had a good time, and you could tell that he was getting along with Ruth magnificently. As Daryl stood at my door to say goodnight, he mentioned that he was leaving on Saturday to head back to college. This was to be his last term before he was done with college. He had loaded up his credits so that he could graduate early, so by spring break, he was finished. That was impressive. He would be able to get a jump on any of the jobs for college students since he will be home earlier. As we stood at my front door, he gently took my hand into his and told me how much fun he had tonight. Daryl asked if he could keep in touch with me until he got back for spring break.

"Sure, that would be great," I responded, not really expecting too much. My face must have reflected what I was thinking. Daryl looked deeply in my eyes and assured me that he would want to stay connected. He leaned in to give me a hug, which was unexpected and awkward. He felt my awkwardness and wrapped his arms around me even tighter. I felt my body relax as though Daryl was mentally willing me to accept his hug. Daryl whispered in my hair that he was going to miss me and quickly released me. I could tell that my face was turning pink and I just nodded my head. Daryl turned and walked away with a backward wave of his hand. That was the strangest farewell that I have ever had.

As I entered my house and flipped the lights on, Angela was sitting on the sofa grinning from ear to ear. "How was your night?" as her giggles pealed out. I rolled my eyes.

"Do I get any privacy? You know exactly how my evening went." I paused for effect. "It was dreamy," I said with a grin.

"Privacy?" And Angela was gone.

Chapter Twelve

I GOT A CALL FROM DARYL ON FRIDAY, WHICH SURPRISED me since I thought we said our goodbyes on New Year's Eve. He was playing basketball with a bunch of the guys and wanted to know if I wanted to come to the gym to watch and then have pizza afterwards. I really did not have anything going on except an old movie that was playing on the television.

"I will pick you up in a half-hour. Is that okay?" I told Daryl that I would be ready, even though I knew that I had to get my butt in gear to do it. Thank goodness that I already had my shower and I only needed to put a dab of makeup on. The phone rang again, and it was Jeffery.

"Hey, I am playing basketball in a bit and wondered if you wanted to come and watch then have pizza." I began to laugh.

"Is this at the gym on Oxford Street?" I asked.

"Yes, how did you know?"

I laughed again. "Because I was already invited by Daryl to go. He is on the way to pick me up now."

"Cool, see you then." I think that was kind of neat that my brother wanted to invite me. They must be playing together.

As I settled myself into Daryl's car, I mentioned that Jeffery called me about the same game. Daryl laughed. "Well, he is not on my team so I must be playing against him."

"Oh, this is going to be hilarious." I said.

"Who are you going to cheer for?" Daryl asked.

"My brother of course!" Daryl turned on his blinker and pulled to the side of the road. "Just kidding!" I laughed as he pulled back onto the road.

As we got to the gym, the parking lot was full of cars. Everyone was beginning their New Year's resolutions already. Not me, I never made resolutions. It was too depressing when I broke them. I needed to be signed in as a guest at the front desk reception area and that only took a few minutes. While I was doing that, Daryl ran to the locker-room to stow his things in a locker and change his shoes. Apparently, you need to have "basketball shoes" that do not go outside of the gym. I guess they do not want little pebbles to get imbedded into the soles and scratch up the gym floor. When you think about that, it sounds logical.

I had already found a seat in the bleachers when I saw Daryl step on the court. He was walking in with Jeffery, and you could tell that he was teasing him about beating the tar out of him in the game. It was all in good fun and they were laughing about it. Daryl does not know how serious Jeff gets when he plays. He can be quite competitive.

As the game began, I recognize some of the team members from the party the other night. It was a good game but a physical one. I thought basketball was a no-touch game because of the rule about fouls but that is not what it looked like when I was watching. The score was neck and neck.

Jeffery went up for a layup as Daryl was trying to block him. They bounced off each other in midair and came crashing down in a heap. Daryl was trying to untangle himself and was the first to jump up. Jeffery continued to lay on the ground. He was rolling back and forth on his back and obviously in a great deal of pain. His face was wincing and drawn tight in a grimace. Daryl was back down and kneeling by Jeff, asking him where it hurt. I was standing up in the bleachers by then, knowing something was terribly wrong. After a few seconds, I realized that Jeffery could not stand, and I was making my way down the bleachers. I could feel the concern and fright beginning to build inside me.

As I knelt by Jeffery, he said that it was his left knee. "We are going to get you to a doctor. Just hold on for a second." I was trying to decide if he needed an ambulance, but I felt that with all these guys standing around, they could help get him into a car.

Jeffery was sitting up as I asked him again, "Which knee is it again?" When Jeff pointed to his left knee, I naturally put my hand gently on it. Suddenly I felt someone place a hand my shoulder, tap it, and put a bit of pressure on it. There was heat that began to radiate from my shoulder all the way down to the tips of my fingers. My hand began to heat up as it lay on Jeffery's knee. Jeff and I grew silent and we both looked at each other. I turned my head around to see who had placed their hand on my shoulder, but no one standing behind me. We had no idea what was happening to my hand, but there was such heat that was radiating from it. It was not a burning heat.

Jeffery said, "Oh God." I was not sure if he was cussing or praying. I asked if he felt anything happening to his knee and he nodded his head in shock. I kept my hand there until it began to cool off, which was about a minute or two. As I took my hand away, there were tears in Jeff's eyes. We just stared at each other. Finally, someone asked what was going on and it broke the silence that had enveloped us.

Jeff whispered, "My knee does not hurt."

Someone in the back of the crowd asked, "What did he say?" Others were repeating the question until it got to the front of the circle that was around Jeff.

Jeff said louder, "My knee doesn't hurt any longer." Everyone started to talk at once. From exclamations of, 'it feels better' or 'it wasn't really hurt' or 'who is going to sub for this guy?' Everyone had a different opinion, and no one really knew what was happening. Jeffery was helped off the court and was gingerly putting weight onto his leg. He kept shaking his head in disbelief.

Once he was on the bench at the side of the court, he turned to me and asked, "What did you do to my knee? It does not hurt at all. I just can't believe it. What was that heat that happened?"

"Jeff, I have no idea what happened. I just felt my arm get really warm and the heat went into your knee. Was your knee really hurt bad?" Jeff nodded his head in affirmation. "Let's talk about this later when there are not as many people around." Jeff agreed. Jeff had stood up and was carefully walking around the gym. He would lean down once in awhile and feel his knee, as though he was checking to make sure it was in place. The game ended and all his guys came around to see how Jeff was doing. He felt really great, he said, but tired. He had decided not go to the pizza parlor but to head back home. I asked Jeff if he needed any help driving his car and he shook his head no.

Daryl and his team went to their favorite pizza place. It didn't matter what kind of pizza they ordered, I could eat anything. We all enjoyed ourselves and then Daryl drove me home. I was pretty quiet on the way home and was reflecting on what had happened at the gym. Daryl walked me to the door, as usual, but did not get too close since he was still had a shirt wet from sweat.

"Jeffery will be fine," Daryl said. It was perceptive of him to know why I was so quiet. I thanked him for the nice day and asked if we could talk later. "Sure, I will call you later."

I got into my apartment and started heating up water for tea. I wondered if I should "call" on Angela to ask her some questions but was not sure, since she said not to do that all the time. I sat on the sofa with my tea in hand and started mentally go through the scenario at the gym. Of course, I had questions, but I felt that I needed to table them for right now. I would call Jeffery tomorrow to see how he is feeling. I turned on the television and started to watching Elf as it was replayed often over the Christmas holidays. You can't help but be drawn into the movie as you watch Buddy start eating spaghetti with maple syrup poured over it. I could hear myself start laughing at his antics.

The next day, in the early afternoon, I gave Jeff a call. He answered after a few rings but before it went to voicemail. He knew that I would not leave a message since I hate doing that. I asked him about his knee.

"It feels fine. I must not have really hurt it. I guess I have a tendency to recover quickly," Jeff chirped. He sounded like he didn't have a care in the world and nothing had happened.

"But what about your knee? You really did hurt it. And what about the heat you felt? I am still processing what that was all about. Any ideas?" I asked.

"I don't know about the heat thing. There must be a logical explanation why your hand was warm. But I am fine now. Will I see you Sunday for dinner?" Jeffery inquired. He was literally blowing past all my questions and concerns about what happened. He changed the subject rapidly. Was he living in a fantasy world? Or maybe I am and don't know it.

We chatted a few minutes and hung up. After the call ended, I realized that I didn't ask him about Ruth. That can wait until Sunday.

But it was really bugging me that Jeff had dismissed the whole accident with his knee and he insisted that it was not hurt. Is Jeff just a big baby? No, I don't think so because I remember him breaking an arm when we were kids and he was a remarkably tough kid. But that means that this whole thing has turned upside down for me. Did I imagine the heat? I pulled my fingers through my hair as I groaned in frustration. There are days that I think I am going nuts! And it all started when Angela showed up. Do I need to look into the fact that I may be schizophrenic?

"No, you are not," said Angela as she sat on top of my table in the corner of the room. I looked over at her and blew out a breath of frustration. I made the sign of grabbing my neck as though I was choking myself, with my tongue hanging out of my mouth. Angela threw back her head with a laugh.

"This is what I am feeling! I feel like I am swimming under water and trying to grasp some air. I am drowning with things that are happening to me. Help me! I need help understanding. And are you sure that I am not mentally ill?"

"I am sure, Susie, you are not ill," said Angela. Just then, there appeared a magnificent looking guy next to her. He had longish blond hair and he had chiseled features, and he had no hair on his face. His eyes were piercing and seemed to see right into your soul. Thinking back, I am not sure what color they were, but I think they were blue or gray. Wait a minute! He looked familiar! I think he was that guy that Angela was with the time I saw them on the sidewalk. I thought he was her boyfriend. I was totally tongue-tied. I was not sure what to do but give him a little wave, like I was in grade school again. I inwardly did an eyeroll, like I was reduced to being a young girl again, clumsy and shy. Angela giggled at my awkwardness. I looked at her with a smirk.

"Is this your boyfriend, Angela?" Angela laughed so hard that she fell off the table. The guy was grinning even broader. "What did I just say that was so funny? You mean, no he isn't?" Angela was pretending to roll on the floor with hilarity, holding her stomach as though it hurt. This time I did an eyeroll for real.

Finally, Angela stopped rolling around on the floor and sat up. "This is one of yours."

"What do you mean one of 'mine'?" I looked from Angela to this hunk of a guy, back and forth, as though I deserved an explanation.

"He is one of your angels. He only shows up once in a while when he needs to be assigned." The hunk did a little wave, that duplicated my previous wave, and was gone.

"I wish you guys would stop doing that! Coming and going in a flash. I have some questions, Angela, and I am really confused. Please sit with me and explain." Angela nodded her head and propped back onto the table. I began to tell her what happened at the gym and how I felt the tap on my shoulder, then pressure, which began heat down my arm. Then I explained about Jeffery's knee and that it did not hurt any longer.

"Was Jeff's knee really hurt? Or is he just a big baby?"

"Yes, his knee was hurt. But God healed it." There was complete silence as I tried to absorb this.

"So, God still heals? Even now-a-days? Don't you still have to pray or bless or….?" I was not sure what I was thinking. I had never heard of God healing in the present day. "Why doesn't Jeffery know?"

"He does, but he does not believe it. He has his own path that he needs to walk with God."

"Really? What is my path Angela? What path am I supposed to be on?" Once again Angela gave a little giggle and pointed up to the ceiling.

"Susie, when are you going to start going to Him? I am not your Bible answer gal. I am here to help you and protect you. I am not here to give you all the answers and take the place of God. If there is ever an entity that is doing that, then it is from the enemy. The world has temples for gods so that you can go there, or they have books that take you on a path away from where the real answers are. Beware of those."

"What books should I be reading then?" As soon as the words left my mouth, I knew what she would say. She gave me one of her looks. "I know, the Bible. But are there other books that I could read?"

"Yes, but do you have a firm foundation yet? Those other books are to be from trusted sources." After a long pause, Angela said, "Susie, you really need to lean on what God says. How is He going to trust you with more if you can not handle the little?" As the reality of what Angela was saying hit my heart, I felt the impact of the truth that was being said. There was so much that has happened lately, that has rapidly been developing, that I have not had a chance to even breathe. Angela could see by my face that her words were hitting the mark. We both looked into each other's eyes and nodded our heads.

This time Angela just faded away slowly instead of poofing away. I had much to chew on. As I sat in my living room, with the light fading away from the day, I realized that I had not taken note of the things that I was learning. I needed to write them down, like a business plan. What are the values that I have learned versus what I am now learning? If I was going to expand my knowledge, what would be my next steps? If I wanted to read other books beside the Bible, what would they be and who would be considered trustworthy? I realized that I needed to make a plan to go to God every morning. And I needed to get a list of questions to ask Angela. Like, who in the heck is that hunk? He is not her boyfriend but he is "one of mine"? One of mine what? A different kind of angel? A light bulb seemed to appear over my head! Ohhhhhh!

The next day, after chewing on this until late the previous night, I was determined to start something new. I guess this was a good way to start the new year, with a few journals. Instead of doing resolutions, I was starting a new journey. I walked down to the local store. They had school supplies still available and I bought a bunch of journals, five in all. Nothing fancy, but in different colors. I walked back to the apartment on this crisp clear day. I was feeling good about this.

I cleared off the kitchen table and spread the journals out on it. I made a title for each of the journals. They were basically listing the questions I had asked myself last night. One was titled, "Questions to ask Angela." I wrote questions, and planned to write the answers in this book when I received them. I set that journal aside and immediately picked it back up. I crossed out the word "Angela" and left the word "questions". I realized that these would also be questions for God. The other journal had "Books to Read" labeled on it. I would put the books that people recommended for me to read. The next journal was labeled "values," and another was labeled, "Bible." I think I will write down verses that pop out to me. I spent the day writing and putting my thoughts into the journals. The hours flew by and I was please with what I had accomplished.

I checked my phone and realized I must have silenced it because I had missed several phone calls. Two were from Daryl and they had gone to voicemail, and one was from my mother and another from Jeffery. I checked my voicemail from Daryl. One said that he wanted to talk to me, and the other was from him saying goodbye as he was getting on the airplane. I suddenly had this sinking feeling that I had mixed up on my days. Is today Sunday? Mom's voicemail was for me to stop at the store for her and Jeffery's was about me being late for dinner. Oh gosh! I checked my watch. I would be a little late but I could make it. I called mom right away and told her that I mixed up my days. Does she still want me to pick up the butter? She said no, she got it taken care of but to get my butt over there.

Barbara Vogel

I grabbed my purse and coat and quickly and ran out the door, locking it behind me. Where was my mind lately? As I drove over to my parent's house, I thought about Daryl's farewell message. It had an edge of frustration to it, that I did not answer his call. I was not too keen on a long-distance relationship, and I felt that it was not the right time to be in a relationship. He was a friend, let's just leave it at that. There has got to be tons of girls at his college.

I arrived at Mom and Dad's in record time. All the traffic lights were in my favor. As I pulled to the curb, I noticed that Mary's car was at the house. Cool! I opened the front door and dad huffed, "Finally!" I apologized profusely at forgetting and stopped short when I saw Damien sitting in the lounge chair in the corner of the room. Mary was sitting on the arm of the chair with her arm around his shoulders. Both of them smiled up at me.

"Hi Damien. Welcome again," as I smiled at Mary. What is it that creeps me out about this guy? Stop it Susie, as if I was mentally talking to myself. As Angela said, he is one of God's children too. I needed to try to be nice to him. Obviously, Mary likes him a lot.

We all gathered around our assigned seats at the dining table and began to sit down. Mom had already placed all the food on the lazy susan. I expressed my apology again to mom and asked her about her New Year's Eve, if she had any resolutions. Mom did not have anything exciting to say and I already knew about her non-resolution resolutions. I must have gotten my thoughts of resolutions from her since she did not make them either. We talked about the party that Jeffery and I went to over at Daryl's house. I knew enough not to ask him about Ruth while we were at the dinner table.

Mary mentioned that Damien was about to start a big project that should be coming to fruition in the springtime. Mary nudged Damien into speaking. He explained that he was starting a conference retreat and spa center. Mom thought this was amazing and she gushed her excitement. He explained that not only will he have a spa, but also exercise like yoga, inner healing, and nutrition.

"We will have a gift shop where you can buy products and books, and things that could be used at the center. For example, workout clothes and yoga mats, healing rocks and crystals. Eventually I would like to have a restaurant or deli on the property," Damien shared. "We will also have a large room where we can have speakers come to the conference center."

"Wow." I exclaimed. "This is a massive project. Do you know where you are doing this? Do you already have a building or a piece of property?"

Damien began to explain his business plan and the location. He had partners that were helping financially and strategically with the property and the building plans. The property was located out of town in a large, wooded area, in a country-type setting. It is by Bridal Veil Falls and attendees will be out in nature, walking the trails, going to the waterfalls, and mediating in peace.

"That is really interesting." I said with encouragement. "So, you will break ground in the springtime? When will the project be finished?"

"Yes, we will be groundbreaking in April, hopefully, if everything is on target. We are hoping that most of the project could be completed by the end of the summer. I know there may be hiccups, but I will be onsite and making sure that everything is going as planned," said Damien. As Damien spoke of his new project, his eyes became alive and intense. You could feel the passion that he had for this project.

"And what will be your role once the project is completed?" I asked. Damien stared into my eyes. I was not sure if he was challenging me or whether he was trying to read my thoughts. I was not challenging him but I was obviously curious, since he was dating my sister. I shifted my body position in the chair and gave him a disarming smile. And Damien smiled back at me. Mary must have felt the slight tension in the room and piped up to explained that Damien was a teacher in inner healing and yoga. She bragged that he had so many talents, like management skills and now is the project manager for this large endeavor. With Damien's eyes still locked onto mine, I replied, "That is fabulous. Congratulations."

I wanted to change the subject, so I said the first thing that came into my head. "Jeffery had his knee healed yesterday." As soon as the words were out of my mouth, I knew I had made a mistake. The scrape of the forks on the plates stopped moving.

Jeffery cleared his throat, "It wasn't a healing. I probably didn't hurt it as bad as it first felt like." Jeffery gave me a look as though as to say, 'why the heck did you bring this up?' I gave him a shrug of my shoulders, as though to say "sorry."

Mary was on this subject like a wolf chasing a rabbit. "What do you mean, Jeff? How did you get hurt and what exactly happened?" Jeffery was visibly uncomfortable and explained what happened. I would pop into the conversation with a few details. As Jeffery wound down the events, he seemed to want to bypass the details of my hand becoming hot on his knee. Damien caught the missing details.

"Why did you say there was a healing, Susie?" looking straight at me.

"Well, my hand was hot when I touched his knee. I am not sure what went on, but I am really thankful that Jeff is okay. It could have been a bad accident," trying to deflect the attention from me.

Damien was intrigued. "Was your hand hot before you touched his knee or while you touched his knee?"

Jeffery abruptly got up from his chair. "Let's not talk about this. I am doing great and basketball can be a pretty physical sport. My knee is fine, thankfully." The subject was closed as far as he was concerned.

Mother jumped up and asked who would like pie? Mary had brought desert and of course everyone said yes for a slice. Jeffery made an excuse as to why he had to leave soon after the dinner was complete. I said I would do the dishes, but I knew I wanted to leave after that. Damien offered to help clear the dishes and told Mary to go relax with her parents. I thought that it was nice of him to do that.

As I began to scrape and pile the dishes into the sink, Damien was making trips back and forth from the dining table. After the table was cleared, he asked where the containers were to put food into the refrigerator. I pointed to a cupboard and he began to put the leftovers into containers. We worked in silence for a while, but I could tell that Damien wanted to talk.

"Susie, I am very interested in the warm hand healing. Could you explain that to me one more time." I skimmed over the details of the incident to him.

Damien said, "I feel that you might be able to heal. Have you ever investigated this before? I have several books about the phenomenon that you experienced. There are people who heal through their hands and they say that their hands become warm when they do it." Damien was looking intently at me. He had the most gorgeous eyes. Damien reached up and put a lock of hair that was flopping in my face and put it behind my ear. I was suddenly feeling this connection towards him and was drawn towards the attention that he was giving me. Damien smiled sweetly. "You are beautiful." As Damien said that, a slight puff of gray haze came out of his mouth. I suddenly dropped the dish I was holding, and it broke with a big bang. The connection was broken. I gasped at the broken dish and also for what just happened in the kitchen. I ran off to get the broom and to collect myself.

By the time I returned with the broom, Mary was in the kitchen, since she heard the noise of the broken dish. She asked I was okay, with concern on her face. I told her I was not hurt or cut. I had my head down and was concentrating on sweeping up the glass fragments. I did not want to look at Mary or Damien for fear there would be guilt all over my face.

"I've got this. You guys go watch television and I'll be out in a second," I mentioned. They readily agreed and I needed to collect myself. I could feel myself getting angry and disgusted with myself, as if I would fall for Mary's boyfriend. What was that all about anyway? I was shocked at my own behavior. This was not like me! I hurriedly finished with the dishes and started the dishwasher. I blew out a breath to steady myself as I walked out to the living room.

"I forgot that I need to call a friend when I get home, so I need to take off. Thanks again mom for a great dinner. Maybe I can cook the next time." Mom gave me a look of disbelief. Now I must be scaring her since I have never offered that before. Actually, I was scaring myself since I don't know how to cook! I really must be losing it!

While I drove home, I was mentally reliving what happened in the kitchen. Damien said that I was beautiful. Geez. But I could not let go of the gesture of putting my hair behind my ear. It was like....intimate. But he is Mary's boyfriend! I waffled between being enamored with Damien and being disgusted and angry with myself, and him.

Obviously, the friend I needed to call was Angela but she did not answer, even after several times of me calling out to her. I paced around the front room. Finally, I told myself I need to stop this obsessing. I turned on the TV and was flipping through channels. I landed on a non-descript show about attorneys. I just needed to give my mind a rest. I was really getting into the plot, when one of the characters was introduced. His name was Damien! I threw up my hands and turned off the television. Geez.

Damien slipped into my dreams that night. I woke up exhausted. The workday was a blur. I think I was coming down with something and I felt unwell. When I got home from work, I ate chicken noodle soup and got ready for bed. As I was washing my face, I looked deeply into the mirror. I felt numb. "Lord, what is happening to me?"

My routine for the following week was eat, sleep and work. My thoughts would constantly drift to Damien and I would try to shove them away. I was working fine while I was at my job, but I felt sad when I got home. I had no boyfriend and I realized that I wanted one. I thought of Daryl, but he was away, and besides we are just friends. Another week had passed, and I was thankful that it was Friday. I finished up my projects and wished Mr. Mack a good weekend. He asked if I was feeling okay. He must have noticed that I had the doldrums. I assured him that I was doing alright. I will be resting the whole weekend and should be as good as new on Monday. That was nice of Mr. Mack to even notice.

I rested most of Saturday. I called mom to see if she wanted me to make dinner for tomorrow, since I promised. She assured me that it was not necessary. She already had a pot-roast ready to go into the crockpot. I offered to make dessert. After the phone call, I realized that I was actually excited to go to my parent's house tomorrow. I wonder if Damien will be there?

I went to the grocery store, and wandered the aisles deciding what to fix for dessert. I wanted to impress everyone with my dessert making skills. And when I thought of everyone, I was thinking of Damien. I was also picking up things for the rest of the week to make for my meals. As I was looking over the apples in the bin, there was a "hello" over my shoulder. I turned and came face to face with Damien. He laughed at the surprise on my face.

"What are you doing here? Is this the grocery store you normally shop at?" I asked. Damien shook his head no.

"Do you have time for a cup of coffee?" he asked. There was a Starbucks coffee in the corner of the grocery store. I nodded my head with a smile. I looked into my basket to make sure there are not any perishables that would melt and there was not.

"How about having coffee now and then I can finish shopping after?" I said. He readily agreed and we walked over to the coffee shop. He asked me what I wanted to drink and mentioned for me to find a table. I found a table and began to watch him talk to the barista with ease. He had a fluid easy going manner that I had not noticed before. I would describe it as elegant. He wore a long dark coat that was quite stylish with jeans and a red dress shirt.

He brought our coffees over and we began to chat as though we had known each other for a long time. The conversation flowed into several different subjects. We talked about education, work, travel, and a bit of politics. We were surprised to find out that we had talked for two hours when we checked the time.

"I am so glad to have run into you Susie. This was really fun. We should do it again sometime. Would you mind if I got your phone number? I am serious about the suggestion that you could maybe work at the confer-ence center. I really do think you have a healing ability that you need to learn more about." I hesitated about giving Damien my phone number. What would be the harm? He watched my hesitation. And he gave me a wide grin when I asked for a pen to write it down. As I was handing him the paper with my number on it, he took my hand and held it for a few seconds. I looked from my hand to Damien's face. His face was inviting and hopeful. I smiled and pulled away.

As I walked away from Damien to finish my shopping, I realized that I had not thought of Mary once during our coffee time. I felt a pang of guilt but quickly waved that away. Hey, I was just being friendly to someone I knew.

The next morning, I felt excitement to go to my parent's for dinner. I knew it was because I wanted to see Damien again. I was careful to make the dessert and hoping he would like it. I arrived a little early to help mom with the dinner preparations. And as expected Damien and Mary arrived shortly after I did. Mother said that Jeffery called, and he was unable to come so when I set the table, it was minus his place setting. It was then that I realized that I had missed church, not only his church but I didn't attend anywhere.

The conversation flowed easily, and we talked about the homeless pop-ulation that was beginning to overflow our city's streets. There were differences of opinion. Mary said that we should leave them alone and let them camp out wherever they want, and my dad's vocal opinion was to have the police arrest the vagrants or at least make them move out of the eyesight of the general population. I did not have an opinion formed, as of yet. I know I did not like them on the streets, but I also did not have a solution. I felt that until you have a solution, you can't complain or voice an opinion.

I offered to do the dishes and Damien said he would be happy to clear the table. Mary said she could help also, but he hugged her and suggested she sit with her feet up and relax. I proceeded to scrape the dishes and pile them into the sink. It was the same routine as always. Damien unloaded the dining room table and started to get the containers out of the cupboard. It was like a repeat from last week but this time we were joking and laughing. We were having a great time. There was a time that Damien spilled some gravy, and made a joke about it that made me laugh. I laughed hilariously and grabbed his arm. Just then, Mary walked in.

Chapter Thirteen

DAMIEN DID NOT MISS A BEAT AFTER MARY WALKED through the kitchen door. "Hello there, come help," said Damien. As for me, my face must have registered guilt. Mary looked from Damien to me and back again.

"Susie, why don't you go put your feet up and I will finish the dishes." I nodded and almost bowled her over in my haste to get out of there. It felt like I was violating Mary's trust in our new friendship. Had I destroyed the friendship that was beginning to blossom between us? But I was not doing anything wrong. She must understand that, right? For the rest of the evening, as we all sat around to watch television, the atmosphere seemed a strained. After the program, I couldn't to get out of the house fast enough.

After I got home, I made myself a cup of tea. What was I thinking? Joking around with Damien like that. My phone rang and it was Damien on the other end of the line. He wanted to apologize for making me uncomfortable. He said, "Everything is fine with Mary and I told her that she misunderstood about us joking around." I felt relieved about that.

"I don't want any trouble between my sister and I." He understood and we chatted for almost an hour. The more we talked on the phone, the more relaxed I became. As we were signing off our conversation, Damien mentioned that it was easy to talk to me.

"Susie, you have a way that makes me at ease with you. I am not usually comfortable around other women, but it is different with you. Besides, you are easy on the eyes." Wow, I had never heard that before. What a compliment. I mumbled my thanks and said goodbye.

As I was getting ready for bed, the phone rang again. It was Damien. I was surprised that he called me back.

"Susie, would it be presumptuous of me to ask you out for coffee again? With this building project, there are some questions I would like to ask attorneys but do not know anyone in this area.

"Sure. We could meet downtown at lunchtime at the coffee shop on Main and Washington. I will send you the address. I think I can get out of the office around 12:15." I think he was pleased that I consented.

We met right on time the next day. I was feeling good and anticipating the meeting with glee. Even though it was a business meeting, I was excited to be seeing Damien again. He was already at the coffee shop, had ordered our coffee, and was sitting at a table in the corner. He had a set of architecture plans laying on the table, unrolled before him. When he saw me, he rolled up the plans and stood to greet me. As I extended my hand to greet him, he grabbed my hand and instead of shaking it, he brought it into his body in order to bring me closer to himself. Damien leaned in and gave me a peck on the cheek. I must have blushed because he chuckled. He did not seem to mind that I was uncomfortable.

As we sat and sipped on the coffee, we talked about his vision of the conference center. He pulled his chair next to me so that he could unroll the plans on the table, so that both of us could see them at the same time. As he was showing me the plans, I could hardly concentrate since he was so close to me. His knee was resting against mine, but I did not want to move it. Soon, he had his arm around the back of my chair, drawing me into his conversation and pointing things out on the plans. His nearness was unsettling, but I did not want it to stop. I loved the attention I was receiving from him. He would reach up and play with my hair once in a while. It was intoxicating. Before I knew it, the alarm on my phone rang that my lunch hour was over, and I needed to get back to work. I rushed out of the coffee shop with a wave of my hand.

While I was walking back to work, I had realized that we did not talk about any legal information that Damien wanted. Did he want to meet me just to show me the plans? Why was he attracted to me and vice versa? And just then I realized that I put into words that I was attracted to him. Oh crap, what about my sister? I really need to think about this.

The rest of the day was a blur. I got home and started making dinner. I called upon Angela again with no response. I was beginning to feel uneasy about the events that were happening. And there was my sister that I needed to consider. She obviously liked Damien. I could see the hurt in her eyes when she entered the kitchen. But what about me? Yes, what about me. What was I thinking, getting involved with her boyfriend? It was nice to be getting attention from an attractive man, but I had always thought there was something off about him. Am I playing with fire? But I felt like such a rebel being sneaky, in a rebellious kind of way. There was a sense of exhilaration and excitement with getting away with something. But then again, he was bringing up these feelings that I thought were long dead, like the thought that someone finds me attractive. It made my insides flutter. I was literally weighing out positives and negatives with Damien about our "relationship." We did not even have a relationship, but it seems to be heading that way. He likes me, that is obvious, but is he a player? Could be. I spent the rest of the evening thinking, weighing, and planning a future. Future? What was I thinking? I was getting more and more frustrated with the process. And then I began to play out in my mind the first few times that I had met Damien. With a jolt, I remembered the gray haze that came out of his mouth.

I had not thought of that for a while. Come to think of it, I have not "seen" anything for quite some time. No "creature" on Damien, no shadows, and the most disappointing thing, no Angela. What is up with that? I have tried to call her or connect with her many times, but to no avail. With all of this thinking and weighing out in the decision-making process, it has made me more depressed and exhausted. I am just going to head to bed and start fresh in the morning. I need to make some decisions on how to proceed. I felt that I was at a crossroads, a crossroad in life. There are times in your life that you realize that you are making a major decision that is in front of you. It is like you are in a junction in your life that you can see two possible roads to take. Decision time. Do I make the decision that will make me feel good? I deserve happiness. And I could make Damien happy. We would make a great couple. Or do I make the decision that puts other people first, like Mary? And it may make me feel empty. I felt like things were spinning out of control. I had to put this aside and get some sleep.

I found myself in a house, standing in the middle of a ballroom. It had many rooms leading off this main room. The door to each of the rooms was closed. I looked around the ballroom and it was magnificently decorated. There was a huge table that was heavily laden with delicious food. There were candelabras decorating the table with greenery and fruit mixed into the greenery as decorations. The tablecloth was a fluorescent red with gold trim and delicate themes on the hem. As I approached the banquet table, I could see the decorations on the hem were palm trees and fruit trees. They were swaying as though there was a breeze flowing through them. I was delighted by the imagery. The floor was marble with veins of gold running through it and it reflected the light of an immense chandelier above my head. The ceiling was extremely high and I would estimate at least 40 feet above my head. I had to crane my neck to see the light fixture. The light from the chandelier was bright enough to light up the ballroom, even though it was so high up. I stood in the center of the room, delighted in everything I was seeing. The walls of the room were painted with scenes of other banquet parties and some were scenes of battles. But they seemed to come alive when I began to watch them but would stop once my sight bypassed the scene. I kept turning around and around to see the marvelous ballroom.

At the far end of the ballroom, there was a magnificent chair that was above the main floor. It was on a platform and I felt that it was a throne. It was carved with lions on the arms of the throne and on the top of the chair was carved with the word "HOLY" in gold. I was drawn towards the chair but was unable to move my feet. They were suddenly stuck on the floor as though they were glued. I tried and tried to move my feet to the point of breaking out in a sweat. I felt this panic begin to rise that I needed to move my feet, and could feel this dread begin to rise, as though it was creeping up my feet and legs. As I looked at my legs they were beginning to grow dark as though they were covered in a sludge. I was alarmed that I had contacted a disease and I opened my mouth to scream and nothing would come out. I needed help! One of the doors at the far end of the banquet room opened, and I could hear footsteps coming towards me. I could not turn around to see who was approaching due to my feet being glued down, as I was facing the empty throne chair. Fear was prickling my skin and I was anticipating dread. As this person came up behind me, I felt his breath upon my neck. He came around to face me and it was Damien. I was so relieved! I laughed out loud in my relief and he laughed also. He came forward to kiss me, and it was an amazing kiss. He pulled back and smiled sweetly. He moved in to give me another kiss again and I pulled back slightly to see him better. Suddenly he transformed and became the scariest creature I have ever imagined, with a huge mouth and awful teeth. I was about to be eaten!

I woke up drenched with sweat and shaking. As I put my hand out to get ahold of my water glass on my nightstand, my hand was shaking, and

I slopped water all over my arm. After I stopped shaking a bit, I went into the bathroom and rinsed cold water over my face. As I looked in the mirror, my face was white, almost a gray. I looked ill. I continued to tremble and I grabbed onto the sink. That dream was so real. I made it back to my bed on unsteady legs. I drew my legs up and hugged them. My forehead rested on top of my knees and I began to sob. I sobbed that I was so thankful that the dream was not real, and I cried that the implications of the dream were real. I cried for over an hour. Every time my tears would let up, I would take a breath and they would begin again. It was as though I had no control over my eyes. After an exhaustive hour, I felt that it was finished. I felt exhausted but cleansed. I looked at the time and it was just approaching 4:30 in the morning.

I got up and made a pot of coffee. I felt different but I couldn't put my finger on it. I went to the hallway closet and got out another box of tissues, since I had depleted the box at my bedside. My eyes would still tear up but it was not a gush, like before. The emotions that I had felt were unexplainable. It was as though I was mourning over a loss. I felt that I should call in sick for work and stay at home to think. For the first time, in an exceptionally long while, my eyes fell on my Bible. I had ignored all nudging to read in that book lately. I felt far away from God. I wondered how that had happened. Did I move away from God or did He move away from me? My tears gushed out in a flow at that thought. Am I losing it? I felt like I was in a storm that could not be controlled. Yes! That is the feeling I was experiencing, the feeling of being out of control.

I flipped open the Bible and it landed on the story of Jesus sleeping in the boat during a huge storm. I began to chuckle at the hilarity of God. He brought this story to me, I just knew it. His friends were frightened in the storm. These are the guys that basically lived on the sea, fishing all the time. They must have experienced storms before this one, but for some reason they were afraid of this particular storm. They woke Jesus up, frightened that they were going to drown. I wondered why they would have woken Him up? Did they believe that He would be able to fix it? Or, that they would disturb His sleep and He could be frightened with them? The fishermen were shocked that Jesus could calm the winds. So why awaken Him? Were they upset that He could sleep through the storm? So many questions. And Jesus asked the disciples one question, where is your faith? Where is MY faith? Once again, my tears flowed! I could tell that this was going to be an exhausting day.

I had my head in the Bible for most of the morning, reading and writing in my journals. I was writing thoughts that spun around in my head and questions that were coming up. I felt that if I could write the questions down, that the Lord would eventually answer them.

As the noon hour approached and I was still in my pajamas, the phone rang. I could see that it was Damien. I did not answer it. I just watched it ring and go to voicemail. About a half-hour later, it rang again. It was Damien. I did not want to talk to him until I had settled in my mind and my heart what I wanted to say to him. In a weird way, I felt the desire to talk to him ebbing away.

I took a long hot shower, cleansing myself of the sweat and fright of the earlier nightmare. I stood in the shower and thanked God for hot water. I felt the water splash down on my head and run down my face and shoulders. I could feel the tension begin to leave my body. I stood there until the water was no longer hot. I did not want to leave this luxurious cocoon of warmth. I opened the door to the shower to grab my towel and wrapped it around me. As I stepped out into the fog of the bathroom steam, there stood Angela.

I was shocked. I'm not sure if I was more shocked that she was in my bathroom or that she had actually came to see me. "Angela, where the hell have you been? I have tried to call you. I have had a terrible time, and I needed your help."

"Hell?" Angela said with a raised eyebrow. I suddenly knew I should be contrite. "Actually," Angela said, "You needed the Father's help. I am glad that you finally decided to connect with Him." And she proceeded to walk through the bathroom door.

"Wait!" I yelled. I rushed out of the bathroom to an empty room. "You have not been around to answer my questions." I said with exasperation.

From the living room, Angela's voice rang out. "I am not a machine that you can put a quarter into and get an answer." I ran out to the front room. She was not there. Grrrrr. I growled in frustration. But, was I frustrated with Angela or frustrated with myself? Was I trying to "put a quarter in" so that I could get the answers quickly and bypass the process of getting the answers? Oh dang, I think I just realized something huge. The process. There is something about the process that I would be learn-ing. It is not like a high school test where you need the correct answer, but it is the process of searching out the answer. And the assurance of receiving the answer from the Author. It was like a puzzle piece that fell into place. Excellent.

As the day wore on, I felt a shedding that was occurring. That is the only word that I could think of, that it felt like a shedding. It was layers peeling off of me that was happening. I think things were happening to my thinking process. They were changing, it was being refined and redirected. With each additional revelation, more questions would surface. I felt that I had accomplished quite a lot for the day, but I also felt that there was a huge expanse that was still untouched. Could I ever get all the answers that I want?

And there I go on another rabbit-trail. What is it that I really want? I began to make a list of things that I want. It was like making a Christmas list. I want to buy a house with bigger closets so that I can fill them with new clothes. A new car would be great, one of those fancy ones that do not use hardly any gas. My list went on, but then stalled. What do I REALLY want? As I thought about it longer, I realized it had nothing to do with physical things on the "Santa" list. What would I put on the "Jesus" list? Now that is a good point! And for some reason I could not start that list yet. I knew that I needed to dig deep to discover those things.

I ate my lunch and knew that I needed to start with the questions that prompted me yesterday. What about Damien? That dream was really awful and realistic.

I picked up the phone to call Jeffery. "Hi Jeff. I have a quick question. Can dreams be a warning from God?" I did not tell him about the dream, and he did not ask. He gave me several references in the Bible of how God talked to the prophets and how He directed things to happen through dreams. I thanked him for the information and hung up. Jeffery seemed to be in a hurry which was fine by me.

For the rest of the afternoon, I looked up the Bible references on how God talked to his people through dreams. Most of stories were about helping with the future, or warning kings of things that were going to happen. Was God warning me about Damien? Was this considered a warning dream? Was Damien really a wolf? A wolf in sheep's clothing? I chucked at my private joke, but realized that it may be true. That saying kept rolling around in my head. Was I to be his next meal? Another chuckle, but then a sense of reality. His next meal... I did not like that thought. And what was the huge beautifully decorated ballroom showing me?

As the day progressed, the "problem" became clearer and clearer. Damien was not for me and I was not sure why or how I was attracted to him in the first place. It was like a spell was put on me. Is there such a thing? Maybe not a spell, but there was evil afoot. I knew that from the first few times that I had met Damien. I got sucked down a road that I should have never have been on. It was one compromising step after another. I would see this while working in the attorney's office, where a client would begin to make a compromising move and it began a snowball effect of mounting problems. And it all came to a decision that should have never been made. When did my steps of compromise begin? I began into search into my memory and search my heart. When did my feelings change? I realized it was back in the kitchen after our meal. Damien was helping me with the dishes. I began to welcome his compliments and his attention. Was there a hole in me that needed filling? Was I ripe for the picking? Was there a "magic-moment" when he would look into my eyes and I would just melt?

I do not believe in magic, but I do know about spiritual forces that can try to manipulate people. It is when you believe a lie that the enemy begins to whisper in your ear. I have seen the creatures that whisper in ears. They are really creepy. And it's kind of fascinating when you see this happening. You want to shout to that person, "wake up!"

It was getting to be evening time, and I was feeling rung out in a good way. I knew that I had accomplished something today and made some huge mileage on my own spiritual walk. As I prepared for bed, I prayed. Yep, me. I prayed. I prayed that I would have a great night's sleep and that I would feel rested when I got up in the morning. I prayed that my conversation with Damien would go well. I needed to figure out what I wanted to say to him. But now, I am toast and ready for rest.

I woke up feeling full of energy. I put my alarm on for earlier than usual so that I could read a chapter in the Bible. I made a commitment that I would do that. I wanted to start the day in the Word.

As I was riding the bus into work, Damien called. He sounded surprised that I answered the phone. "Hi Susie. Are you okay? You didn't answer any of calls yesterday."

"Yes, I am good. In fact, I am really good today," I answered. I did not think I needed to have an excuse as to why I did not answer any of his calls.

"Okay." He exaggerated the word like he expected an answer. Hum, that was interesting. He wanted an explanation. There were a few moments of silence. I think that Damien was perturbed. He is accustomed to women falling all over themselves for him. "I was wondering if we could meet for coffee again. We got all wrapped up in the plans that I was showing you and I forgot to ask you some legal questions."

"I guess we did not get to those questions, did we? How about I make you an appointment with one of our attorneys? The first appointment is at no charge and it is basically finding out if they can help you. As far as having a coffee with you, I think I will bow out. I have been thinking that it is not a good idea for us to meet since you are with my sister."

There was a long moment of silence. "Well Susie, I was going to talk to you about myself and Mary. I am not sure things are going to work out with us and I wanted to ask your advice. I think that there is some electricity between us and I wanted to know if you felt the same thing. Susie, I am attracted to you. There, I have said it." There was a moment of silence as I digested what Damien just said.

"Hold on." I put the phone on my lap. I closed my eyes. Lord, put the right words in my mouth. "Damien, I don't think this will work out. I am on a different trajectory in my life. I spent the whole day yesterday reading the Bible. I am searching out the hidden Truths about God."

"That is what is happening to me too!" Damien had excitement in his voice. "I want to know the hidden truths. I think we could discover these things together. That is why I am putting together this conference center, so that people can discover the god that is within themselves."

Ohhh my Lord! It is obvious that I am getting out of this by the skin of my teeth. Thank you, Lord. I tried to keep my voice calm. "Damien, we are on different paths. I am talking about the Truths of the Almighty God. That is truth with a big "T". I am discovering the love that God has for us. Like a best-friend kind of love. I think Damien, we are on a different wave-length, but we can still be friends. I will see you on Sunday, if you come for dinner. I gotta go, I need to get off the bus now. Bye." As I got off the bus, I let out a big sigh of relief. I am glad that conversation was over.

Chapter Fourteen

DARYL CALLED ME A FEW WEEKS AFTER THE DAMIEN thing, and we had a nice long talk about school and what he does with his leisure time. He said that he had been extremely busy, and he cannot wait to be home for spring-break and to be done with school. We ended up talking for about an hour and a half. The conversation flowed was as though we had no break from each other. I told him about my recent journey with the Lord, Damien, and Mary. He was quiet throughout this big reveal. He asked a few questions, but was genuinely interested in what I was saying. I could tell that Daryl was upset about Damien but I explained that without that encounter, I would not be on the road with the Lord that I was on now. Damien actually made me realize where my heart was positioned. It is hard to explain, but I think I needed to walk through that mess to find out how easily I could go down a slippery slope. We said our goodbyes and said that we would write emails to each other.

Later in the evening, Angela came in to say hello, and we began to discuss the motivation of my heart. Our meetings were infrequent, but the conversations were on a deeper level. And as always, short. There was something that was bugging me lately that I needed to ask Angela.

"Angela, when I was having all that trouble with Damien, why didn't you come and give me advice? You could have saved me a lot of trouble."

"Susie, can you hear yourself? I am not here to "save" you. That is what Jesus does. You could not summon me because of your motivation in your heart. You wanted to be rescued and be told what to do. I answer to our King. He is the One to guide you, but often He does not "tell" you what to do. You have your own free will to make decisions, and He has given you the guidance in the Word to do that. It is also your free will to choose not to rely on what He has given you. I cannot take the place of your will or our King."

"Well, Angela, it would have been much easier for me if I had been warned about Damien," I pouted.

Angela chuckled. "You needed to learn that lesson on your own. As you know, Damien is on a different path. You must pray for him. If he needs help to return to the Father, you may be there to help guide him."

"You mean like you guide me? You mean I will be like his angel?" I said with a laugh.

"NO!" Angela said this with sternness. I was taken back at the intensity of her response. I gulped. "You and I are much different. You have a lot to learn," Angela said with more calmness in her voice.

"I think I almost made a big mistake with Damien. I replay in my mind what happened, and what could have happened." I let out a breath and shook my head at the possible consequences.

"Yes, and look how easily you almost went in a different direction. You must keep your guard up always against the evil one," said Angela.

"You mean Damien?"

"No, Damien is not the evil one. He is one of God's creations. The evil one uses people to do what he wants."

I opened my mouth to ask another question. Angela shook her head. "That is for another discussion." Angela waved a goodbye.

I marveled at how she knew what I was going to ask. She was right. My question would have opened up a whole new sphere of discussions. I needed to dig in the Bible to find how to guard myself. I am beginning to learn that this book has many answers that I could have asked Angela, but I am also learning about the process. I am also seeing that there are layers of things that are being revealed. For example, I could read a scripture and return to that same scripture weeks later and have some-thing else revealed that I had not noticed before. It was a wonder how I missed it in the first place. It was like I needed to learn on one level before I was to learn the next one. I am still trying to figure that one out. But the process has been fun. And with this growing process of reading the Bible, I have begun to see things a little more clearly. But that is a discussion for another time.

THE END

Author Biography

Barbara Vogel has worn many hats during her lifetime and her newest hat is that of an author. For many years she was a Radiology/Diagnostic Imaging supervisor in a large metropolitan hospital in Washington State until she was radically called into a different direction in her life. Her hunger to know more about God and the spiritual realm had landed her in a ministry school in Redding, California where she had radical encounters with Him. Barbara has a passion for travel in any mode that is available. She has traveled to 29 countries and 43 states of the United States and has crossed the country three times on her Harley Davidson motorcycle. Barbara loves adventure but her passion is to mentor students and to bring clarity and breakthroughs for them whether in the school environment or on mission trips.

Look forward to reading her next book: The Basic Guide to the Feeler Gift. This book explores one of the gifts of the Holy Spirit and its multi-dimensional way that God can talk through emotions, atmospheres and why people have this gift. It will give verbiage to this special gift that many of the population have and had difficulty navigating.